# DEATH AT WARBLERS' END

BELLAMY BECK

*To C.W. and Rusty, for introducing me to Frank, Joe, and Nancy all those years ago.*

*And to Connie, for surrounding me with books.*

# CHAPTER 1

*a* July sunrise painted the Adirondack sky purple and orange as eerie wailing sounds echoed across the lake.

"Nothing creepier than loons calling to each other first thing in the morning. Am I right, kiddo?"

I spun around to see a tall, bearded figure shuffle out of the porch shadows into the cool morning air. It was my father, Henry Stillman, sporting his signature look of an unbuttoned flannel shirt over faded overalls. When I was a little girl, I'd started calling him Fuzz because of the beard, and the name stuck. Anyway, he owned Loon Lodge, and thanks to him, I'd spent the last four months coated in dirt, wood stain, and a cocktail of mystery gunk that kept me awake at night.

"Hey, Fuzz." I scooted sideways to make space on the swing. "Take a load off?"

He handed me a mug of hot coffee and plopped down beside me. His companion, a tan-and-white brute of a standard poodle named Charley, stretched out on the porch floor beside us.

The view of the lake was postcard perfect, but as I sipped coffee, all I could think about was the sorry state of the lodge. Harsh Adirondack winters and deferred maintenance had taken a toll.

The lodge's weathered logs begged for fresh coats of stain and sealant, the roof leaked during heavy rainstorms, and the landscaping looked like an overgrown forest. The list of problems ran longer than a squirrel's winter stash list.

Or at least that's what it seemed like when my best friend, Evie Hicks-Turner, and I arrived at the lodge back in March. Fresh off a divorce more than twenty years in the making, I'd left Rochester hoping to spend a relaxing summer in the mountains with Fuzz and my daughter, Maddie, who'd lived at the lodge for the past year.

When Evie and I saw the lodge's condition up close, our plans for a carefree summer flew out the window, replaced by a half-baked idea to give the place a facelift. What started as a simple painting project quickly snowballed into a grand plan to revamp the entire business.

Not that Loon Lodge was just a business. The lodge sat on the shore of Beechtree Lake, between Black Spruce Marsh and miles of state forest. It was constructed in 1910 as a sanatorium for a rich industrialist from New York City. My great-grandfather later purchased it and converted it into a hotel for the waves of tourists who flocked to the Adirondacks throughout the twentieth century.

All told, Stillmans had lived on the property for more than seventy-five years, and the lodge figured prominently in our family history.

In my not-so-humble opinion, it was also one of the best-kept secrets of the Adirondacks. Nestled at the intersection of a forest, a lake, and a marsh, the property offered a convenient getaway for nature lovers.

As avid birders, Evie and I loved slogging through the

marsh to spot an American bittern or trekking nearby forest trails to catch the rhythmic "thunk-thunk" of a pileated woodpecker hammering on a tree trunk. We envisioned transforming the place into a world-class destination for birdwatchers and other nature junkies.

To get the ball rolling, we'd tapped into Evie's Jedi-level marketing skills and organized a weekend birding festival. It was scheduled to take flight in a few days, and we were hoping to attract birders from all over the Northeast.

With luck, attendees would put Loon Lodge on the map by sharing their experiences across the birding communi-ty's massive network of apps, listservs, and social media groups.

"So, Honeysuckle," Fuzz tapped his foot on the porch floor. "Is everything set for this shindig of yours?"

I still couldn't believe he'd convinced my mother to name me after an invasive weed species. Fuzz had always claimed it was because he admired honeysuckle plants' relentless, never-give-up attitude, but his explanation was hardly comforting.

"Nice try," I said, shooting him a friendly glare. "I've gone by 'Honey' since first grade, and there's no turning back now." I took a sip of coffee. "Joking aside, you've got the game plan down, right?"

Fuzz bent over and gave Charley's head a ruffle. "Abso-lutely. But maybe you should give me a recap."

I rolled my eyes. "The festival is on Saturday. We've scheduled conservationists, nature educators, vendors, and a food tent. And Nora Pruitt is our featured speaker."

"Nora's kind of a big deal, right?" I couldn't tell if he was messing with me or truly drawing a blank on our past chats about Nora. In any case, I played along.

"Uh, yeah. She's kind of a celebrity in the birding world, and she has groupies." I had no idea how Evie had convinced

Nora to speak at the festival, but her participation guaranteed a crowd.

Fuzz rubbed his long gray beard. "Well, I guess we're gonna have to buckle down over the next few days to get this place shipshape then."

"Exactly. Guests start arriving Friday. Between now and then, we need to prep guest rooms, spruce up the grounds, and keep plugging away on the facelift. And don't forget, we're having dinner with the mayor tonight."

Fuzz's expression turned sour. "You know how I feel about that woman, Honey. Can't you and Evie handle dinner on your own?"

"Not a chance." I drained the last of my coffee and placed the empty mug on the porch rail. "We need Tawny Walters on our side if we're going to save this place."

The lodge's rundown condition and dismal occupancy rate had recently landed it in the crosshairs of town officials, and the zoning department was starting to ask questions. If we impressed Tawny, maybe it would buy us some time to get the lodge back on track.

"That's not all," I continued. "We invited Tawny and her husband, George, to spend the night so they can really soak up the lodge experience."

Fuzz groaned and turned to Charley. "Eat your Wheaties, buddy. It's gonna be a long day."

FUZZ AND CHARLEY spent the morning and most of the afternoon rehabbing the lodge's great room. Meanwhile, Evie and I whipped up a classic Adirondack spread of wild mushroom soup, pan-seared salmon with lemon-caper sauce, grilled asparagus, and roasted potatoes. No small feat for a couple of culinary-challenged chicks and a commercial stove that was decades past its prime. We even managed to pull together a blueberry cobbler for dessert.

As we waited for our dinner guests in the two-story great room, Evie and I took in the scent of freshly oiled cedar timbers and the glow of the room's rustic chandeliers.

"Don't laugh, Honey," Evie whispered, "but this feels like a fairy tale."

She was right. The great room oozed a special kind of magic. The crackling fire in the hearth, the smell of mushroom soup wafting from the kitchen, the century-old banquet table—everything spoke to the lodge's storied past and future potential as a place for special moments.

"You know, the lodge isn't the only thing looking spiffy tonight. You look amazing!" I said, glancing over Evie's bold pink pantsuit and trendy lavender glasses. She was a decade older than me, but her fashion game was always on point.

I'd abandoned the idea of a cocktail dress and opted for something more low-key: khaki capris and a pastel blue button-up that highlighted my shoulder-length blonde hair and concealed my extra curves. It wasn't as flashy as Evie's outfit, but it was a major upgrade from my typical getup of cargo pants, sneakers, and a t-shirt.

"I don't know, Evie. Maybe I should change into something snazzier."

Evie arched an eyebrow. "Honey, you don't have to change a thing. You're a classic, and you're absolutely rocking that summer mountain-chic look."

"Thanks, Evie." I loved the way she sugarcoated reality for me.

"No Maddie or Liliana?" Evie asked.

I shook my head. "Not tonight. Maddie's on campground patrol, and Liliana's tied up at the Hop House."

Maddie was a rookie New York State forest ranger, and her girlfriend, Liliana, ran High Peaks Hop House, a local microbrewery famous for its wood-fired pizza. They made a cute couple, but between rescuing lost hikers and keeping Beechtree stocked up on craft beer, they didn't have very much spare time.

"At least Maddie's joining us for the birding hike in the morning," I said as I fussed with the appetizer trays on the banquet table. "And Betsy should be here any minute."

Evie wrinkled her brow. "I still don't understand why you thought it was a good idea to invite Betsy. She's so cantankerous."

I reached across the oak tabletop and repositioned the cheese plate for the third time. "I know, but her family has lived next door to the lodge forever, and she's been angling for a dinner invitation ever since her parents passed away. Besides, she knows everything there is to know about Adirondack history, so at least she'll keep the conversation interesting."

"Then I guess we're good to go," she said. "Fuzz checked in Tawny and George Walters a little while ago. Naturally, they requested cabins instead of rooms in the main lodge."

"Cabins, as in more than one?" Each cabin slept eight people and took twice as long to turn over as a room in the main lodge. We couldn't afford to waste time. Not this week.

"Apparently, the husband has sleep apnea," Evie explained as she moved the cheese plate back to its original spot on the table. "They're in Cabin 5 and Cabin 6. Fuzz checked someone else into a cabin too."

"Seriously? I thought we agreed that we aren't taking walk-ins this week?"

Evie shrugged me off. "The guy's harmless, Honey. Apparently, he's in town for a last-minute business trip. Fuzz said he didn't blink when he quoted him the full rate, and he paid for the entire stay up front. In cash."

I wasn't thrilled about turning over another cabin before

the festival, but the lodge could use the money. "Any sign of Nora?"

"Not yet," Evie replied. "She said there's a chance she won't make it until tomorrow."

"Well, remind me to call her first thing in the morning if she doesn't turn up later tonight."

So much for wowing Tawny with a bonafide VIP. Now we'd have to win her over ourselves, and I wasn't crazy about our chances.

George and Tawny finally arrived, decked out and dazzling. Middle-aged with a rapidly receding hairline, George wore a tailored suit and tie. Not to be outdone, Tawny turned heads in a daringly low-cut cocktail dress and dangly earrings that sparkled when she moved. I gave Fuzz credit for wearing his best flannel shirt and slicking back his hair, but now I really wished I'd worn the dress.

My outlook improved as the evening unfolded. Though the mushroom soup was delish, the salmon stole the show. Bottles of wine and Hop House IPAs flowed, and against all odds, everyone seemed to be having a good time.

When Evie and I excused ourselves to dish up dessert, we left George and Betsy engaged in an animated chat about the history of the Adirondack chair. On the opposite side of the table, Fuzz and Tawny were absorbed in their own conversation. I couldn't make out the words, but they were getting along so well that Tawny's annoying laugh felt almost bearable. If it helped the lodge, she could laugh any way she wanted to.

Back in the kitchen, I couldn't contain my giddiness. "Can you believe how fantastic this is going?"

Evie's face broke out in a big smile. "Who knew Fuzz had it in him? And Betsy and George are acting like new besties."

"Don't forget about Tawny," I said, piling generous scoops of cobbler onto dessert plates I'd bought special for the occasion. Then, lowering my voice, I added, "Between you and me, I think she's had one too many."

Evie snickered. "That's not hurting things, either."

As we carried the plates of cobbler into the great room, it was apparent something—or someone—had thrown a wrench in the works. Tawny hadn't budged. She remained seated at the table slurping Chardonnay while George and Betsy sat across from her, staring at their plates. The kicker was Fuzz. He stood towering over Tawny and shouting, his face red as a ripe tomato.

"You've got some nerve," Fuzz yelled, glaring at Tawny. "You think you can stroll in here, drink our wine, and then just destroy everything my family built? Well, think again, sister."

Tawny shrugged her shoulders. "Sorry, Fuzz, but we both know how valuable the lodge is. If it's not me, it's gonna be someone else. You know what they say, better the devil you know than the devil you don't."

"You've got the devil part right!" Fuzz slammed his fist on the table.

The clatter of silverware and glasses hung in the air. Tawny's eyes grew wide as the rest of us exchanged worried glances.

"Let's all take a deep breath. Whatever this is, I'm sure we can work it out," I said, trying to defuse the bomb that had gone off on the first day of festival week.

"Stay out of this, Honey," Fuzz warned. "This is between me and Tawny."

With a sniff, Tawny stood up from the table, slung her purse over her shoulder, and teetered out the front door.

Fuzz stared at Tawny's empty chair, then he called for Charley and stormed out of the room too, slamming the door behind him.

Evie and I traded bewildered looks, both of us at a loss

about what to do next. Finally, George cleared his throat and saved us the trouble of saying something awkward. "Well, that was . . . um . . . exciting," he said, forcing a polite smile. Then he excused himself and followed Tawny and Fuzz out the door.

Betsy pushed away from the table and stood to her feet. "Buckle up, campers, this is about to get ugly. Neither of those hotheads knows how to back off." Polishing off her IPA, she added, "Trust me, the excitement's just getting started."

A weight settled on my chest as the rosy future I'd pictured for the lodge suddenly seemed like a long shot. There was no way Tawny would support our efforts to resurrect Loon Lodge now.

# CHAPTER 2

"*M*orning, sunshine."

I blinked my eyes open and found myself staring at a shirtless Sam Abbott. For a second, I thought I was still dreaming. And if I was dreaming, I didn't want to wake up.

But it wasn't a dream, it was the real deal. Sam, my sort-of boyfriend, stood beside the RV's queen bed, looking even more handsome than usual. I melted every time I saw his tousled sandy hair and laid-back smile. Though we'd only been dating for a few months, he already felt like my favorite sweater. Comfy, welcoming, and always there when you need him.

"What time is it?" I asked, rubbing my eyes.

He glanced at his watch. "Six-thirty. Coffee's made, time to shake a leg."

I yawned and stretched, then dragged myself out of bed toward the smell of freshly brewed coffee in the RV's galley. Pouring myself a cup, I took a moment to savor the taste as I enjoyed the sensation of crisp mountain air flowing in through the screen door.

During the winter months, Sam lived in a small house that he'd inherited from his parents. The rest of the year he lived in his RV, parked on a scenic piece of land he owned just outside of town. I didn't mind the camper. It felt like the cabin Evie and I shared at the lodge, but smaller and with better WiFi.

As the caffeine worked its voodoo, I mulled over the events of the past twelve hours. I'd originally planned to spend the night at Sam's place, but after the dinner debacle, I thought it might be best to stay at the lodge. Evie wouldn't have it, though. She'd promised to check on Fuzz and practically shoved me out the door.

"Sorry I was a downer last night," I said. My mind flashed back to how I'd monopolized our conversation, venting about Tawny and Fuzz.

Sam leaned in, his lips almost touching my cheek. At the last second, he playfully veered away and reached over my shoulder to grab the coffee pot. "I'm kinda bummed I missed dinner. Sounds like it was quite the show," he teased.

"More like a disaster," I smirked. "Fuzz and Tawny's argument ruined the entire night."

Sam topped off his mug and returned the carafe to the cradle. "You have no idea what got Fuzz so riled up?"

"Not really. Tawny mentioned property values and hinted about some plan she had for the lodge, but that's all I know. Betsy was gabbing away with George, so she doesn't know anything either. The only people who really know what it was about are Fuzz and Tawny."

Sam took a sip of his coffee before settling into a seat at the dinette. "I've gotta say, giving Fuzz a night to simmer down shows restraint. Not usually your strong suit," he noted.

"Trust me, I wanted to grill him right then and there, but Evie talked me out of it." It hadn't taken much convincing on

Evie's part. By the time we finished cleaning up from dinner, I'd developed a pounding headache, and listening to Fuzz rage about Tawny would have only made it worse.

I refilled my coffee and settled into the seat opposite Sam in the dinette. "I'll talk to Fuzz today and get to the bottom of it," I said, knowing full well that my plan hinged on Fuzz's cooperation, and that wasn't a slam dunk.

"What's next?" Sam asked.

"We stick to the schedule and hope for the best, starting with a birdwatching hike around the property this morning. What's on your plate today?"

Sam checked his watch. "I need to get going soon. There's an early delivery at the store, and strangely enough, neither of my employees volunteered to wake up early to unload the truck. But if you're up for it, pizza's on me at the Hop House tonight."

"Hawaiian pizza?" I asked, batting my eyelashes like a spoiled teenager.

"The things I do for you, Honey Palmer. Deal."

THE NINE O'CLOCK birdwatching hike started promptly at nine-fifteen, which was right on schedule in the birding community. We'd invited our friend, Wanda Rosenthal, to join us. The owner of Beechtree's Beary Good Cafe, Wanda also served as president of the North Country Fly Girls, a local women-only birding club Evie and I proudly belonged to.

In addition to Wanda, the group of hikers included Evie, Betsy, and Maddie. George showed up too, but there was no sign of Tawny or Fuzz.

"Apologies for Tawny," George said, looking sheepish. "She's probably still hungover from last night."

I waved him off. "No problem, George. Let's get started, and Tawny can catch up if she feels up to it."

With everyone accounted for, I led the group down the winding path along the lake's shoreline. A warm breeze rustled the grass, and the sweet scent of blue flag iris mingled with the smells of damp earth and Beechtree Lake.

As we walked, stillness gave way to a chorus of bird sounds. The telltale tapping of a downy woodpecker drifted from the trees on the other side of the property, while a band of black-capped chickadees filled the air with their cheery "chick-a-dee-dee" calls. Farther down the path, a red-tailed hawk soared overhead, its shrill cry piercing the sky. Maddie pointed out a pair of cedar waxwings perched on a nearby tree, adding their trills to the symphony.

Rounding a corner, we stumbled on a great blue heron wading in the shallows. We watched it snatch a wriggling bluegill from the water. I'd seen dozens, maybe hundreds of herons over the years, but their size and gracefulness always amazed me. George stood transfixed, staring through a pair of binoculars on loan from Maddie.

"Incredible, isn't it," I whispered to George, careful not to disturb the heron. "Nature always finds a way to surprise you."

George's eyes stayed glued to the binos. "I never realized how beautiful they are. And big!" he said, finally breaking away from the heron.

As we pressed on, Wanda spotted a flash of color in the trees. "A scarlet tanager!" she said in a hushed voice. Group members craned their necks to get a glimpse of the little red songbird before it flitted away.

"Wow, that was phenomenal!" I said. "Scarlet tanagers aren't very common around here, even during the breeding season. Let's hope it sticks around for the festival."

"Who's up for checking out Black Spruce Marsh?" I

continued. "We saw some American coots and a belted king-fisher there recently." Turning to George, I explained, "Our part of the marsh is called Warblers' End because warblers tend to perch in the vegetation along its edge. We might even see a common yellowthroat or a black-throated blue warbler today if we're lucky."

The group nodded in agreement, and we set off for the marsh. As we walked, people paired off and chatted among themselves.

"Evie told me things got pretty wild at your dinner party last night," Maddie said, a sly grin playing at the corners of her mouth.

"Wild is one way to put it," I sighed, glancing over my shoulder to make sure the rest of the group was still with us. "Let's just say Fuzz and I have a lot to talk about when I get back to the lodge."

Maddie's face softened. "Hey, cut the guy some slack. You grew up here, but this place is his whole world. It's all he has."

She wasn't wrong. No one wanted to see the lodge restored to its former glory more than me, but Fuzz had devoted his entire life to it. Even so, he owed me some answers about why he had decided to make an enemy of the one person we needed on our side.

I changed the subject rather than getting into it with Maddie. "What's new with you and Liliana?"

Maddie shook her head. "Not much, really. Liliana is working twelve-hour shifts at the Hop House, and I'm working extra hours too. We haven't had much time for each other lately, but we both have tomorrow night off."

"Date night?" I asked.

Maddie's face lit up. "You know it, and I can't wait."

As we approached the marsh, a metallic rattle sliced the air. I turned to Maddie. "Did you hear that?"

"It's the kingfisher," she answered, eyes sparkling.

I called the group together and pointed in the direction of the kingfisher's call. "We have a bird blind at the edge of our property overlooking the marsh. Let's make our way over there and see if we can sneak a look at the kingfisher."

We crept toward the northeastern edge of the property, our casual chatter replaced by the sounds of croaking frogs and buzzing insects. The marsh stretched before us, the morning sunlight glinting off its murky water. At the edge of the marsh, the blind—a dilapidated wooden shack—stood sentinel.

As we got closer, a flash of white caught my eye. I trained my binoculars for a better view and instructed Maddie to stay with the group.

Inching forward, I saw that it was a white lace nightgown, soaked through. More alarmingly, it looked like the nightgown's owner was still wearing it. The head and shoulders were submerged in the water, but the torso and a pair of legs were clearly visible on dry land.

My stomach lurched as I realized I was looking at Tawny's lifeless body.

# CHAPTER 3

$\mathcal{T}$he discovery of Tawny's body at Warblers' End sparked a flurry of activity. Evie took charge and led the group back to the lodge while Maddie and I stayed behind to watch over the body and call 911. It was a grim task, but someone had to do it.

George seemed numb. He didn't even protest when Maddie said we needed to leave Tawny's head submerged in the water to preserve the scene. He just followed the rest of the group back to the lodge, his face blank and expressionless.

A few minutes later, a pair of EMTs arrived followed by Beechtree's police chief, Big Ted Dibley, and his two deputies. Big Ted was a character, a compact and bony man who compensated for his small stature with a massive ego and an insistence that people include the word "big" when they addressed him. Even though the police chief's position was only part-time, Big Ted swaggered around Beechtree like Roy Scheider in Jaws, constantly on the lookout for threats to the community—real or imagined.

"The medical examiner is on the way," Big Ted

announced as his deputies cordoned off the area around Tawny. "The EMTs will stand by until he's finished, then they'll remove the body. The scene is secure, and we'll take it from here."

I wanted more details. "What can you tell us?"

"What can I tell you?" Big Ted parroted. "She's dead."

Maddie cut in before I lost my temper and said something I'd regret. "I think my mother is asking whether you have any idea what happened here."

"You tell me," Big Ted said, pulling a notepad from his pocket. "How did you know the victim?" I didn't like the way he emphasized the word "victim." He made it sound menacing.

"I wouldn't say we knew her, per se," I explained. "Tawny and George were guests at the lodge last night."

"Guests? You mean they spent the night here?" Big Ted scribbled something in his notepad. "That's weird. They only live a few miles away."

"Actually, it's not weird at all," I added as I tried to sneak a peek at what he'd written down. "The Walters were guests at a dinner we hosted last night, and we comped them a couple of cabins so they could see the work we're doing on the lodge firsthand. You probably heard about the birding festival this Saturday."

"I might've heard something about it." Big Ted shifted his attention to Maddie. "Were you there?"

"No, I was patrolling the campground. I'm a forest ranger," Maddie replied.

Big Ted snorted dismissively. "Forest ranger, huh? I hope you don't have any ideas about sticking your nose where it doesn't belong. Just remember that you're in Beechtree now, and this is Beechtree PD's jurisdiction."

Maddie's cheeks flushed red. "Understood."

Part of me wished she would have let him have it, but I

was glad she held back. We couldn't afford to make enemies with the local police right now.

"In addition to the Walters, Evie Hicks-Taylor and my father, Fuzz Stillman, were also at the dinner," I said.

"You mean Henry?" Big Ted asked.

"Yes. Henry Stillman," I confirmed, "but he goes by Fuzz. And our neighbor, Betsy Fitzsimmons, was there too."

"Anyone else?" he pressed.

"Not at the dinner," I answered, "but we had another guest staying in one of the cabins. I have his information back at the lodge office."

"My girlfriend, Liliana, also lives on the property," Maddie offered. "She was working in town at the Hop House and came back to our cabin around eleven o'clock."

Big Ted stopped writing and looked up from his notebook. "I see," he said, casting bigtime shade in Maddie's direction.

"Is there a problem?" I snapped.

"That's what we're trying to determine, ma'am," he replied, unfazed by my sharp tone. "Was there alcohol at this dinner of yours?"

"Yes, we served alcohol at dinner," I shot back. "Halfway through the appetizers, we decided to toss back shots of vodka and tequila out of teapots. Let's keep that our little secret, though."

"So that's a yes on the alcohol?" he asked, his pen hovering over his notepad.

"We served wine and beer," I answered.

Big Ted perked up. "Do you have a liquor license for that?"

"We don't need one," Maddie interrupted. "The Walters were guests at a private dinner, not customers."

Big Ted looked disappointed, but he accepted Maddie's explanation and moved on. Score one for the good guys.

Then he asked about Tawny's alcohol consumption, and I admitted that she'd drank a little too much wine, leaving the main lodge tipsy around eight-thirty.

"All right, we're almost done here," Big Ted said. "Just a few more questions for now. You mentioned that the Walters stayed in separate cabins. They're married, right? What's that about?"

"As far as I know, they are married," I explained. "But Tawny wanted separate cabins because George has sleep apnea and uses one of those machines at night."

"That's weird, too," Big Ted muttered, scratching more notes in his pad. "I have sleep apnea, and my wife hasn't banished me from the bedroom."

"That's surprising," I wisecracked.

Big Ted sent another disapproving look my way. "In any case, we might have a state police forensics team go through their cabins. That means the Walters's cabins are off limits until I give the all clear." He flipped his notepad closed and returned it to his back pocket. "Obviously, we're still in the preliminary stages of the investigation," he continued, "but dollars to donuts, we're looking at an accidental drowning."

I wrinkled my eyebrows. "Really? How can you be sure it was an accident?"

"We can't be completely sure until the medical examiner files his report, but alcohol plays a role in most accidental drownings." Big Ted adjusted the oversized utility belt on his bony hips. "Based on the position of the body, my guess is that she wandered around intoxicated, became disoriented, and ended up face down in marsh water."

Maddie agreed. "He's right. Alcohol is a factor in a lot of park drownings. And I did find an empty wine bottle near the blind. It's entirely possible Tawny got turned around and fell into the marsh."

I nodded, even though I had a feeling there might be more to the story.

Big Ted's voice softened. "Listen, let's wait for all the evidence to come in. Once we get the medical examiner's report back, we'll have a better idea what really happened." He placed a knobby hand on my shoulder. "Give us some time to piece it all together, and we'll find answers."

"Let us know if there's anything we can do to help," I said.

"Count on it. And remember: no one goes in those cabins without my say-so." Big Ted started to walk away, then turned around. "There is one more question I need to ask. Due diligence and all."

"Sure, no problem. What is it?"

"Did anything unusual happen at that dinner of yours?"

MY MIND RACED as Maddie and I made our way back to the lodge from Warblers' End. Tawny's death was tragic, no question, but something about Big Ted's theory just didn't add up for me.

"Maddie, put on your forest ranger hat for a minute," I said. "Why would Tawny wander around Black Spruce Marsh in her nightgown?"

"I hate to admit it, but I think Big Ted's right," Maddie answered. "Tawny probably wandered out of her cabin drunk, got lost in the dark, and fell into the marsh. I expect the medical examiner's report will confirm his theory." She paused. "Now, I've got a question for you."

"Fire away."

"Why did you lie to Big Ted?" she asked. Her voice had a stern edge. It reminded me of the tone I'd used when I caught her fudging the facts about her fourth-grade report card.

I blinked, surprised. "Wait, what? I told him everything I know," I said, feeling a flush creep up my cheeks.

She sighed. "When Big Ted asked if anything strange happened at dinner, you conveniently skipped over Fuzz and Tawny's argument."

"Okay, so I didn't tell him everything," I admitted, avoiding her gaze. "But it's not a lie. We had a nice dinner, Tawny excused herself, and everyone else left shortly after. That's all true."

Maddie came to an abrupt stop in the middle of the path. "Don't play games, Mom. I'm trying to help you. What happened between Fuzz and Tawny?"

I hesitated. "I honestly don't know. One minute they were chatting it up like old friends, and the next minute they were sworn enemies."

A worried look crossed Maddie's face. "I know you didn't want to make Fuzz look bad, but now you've made Big Ted suspicious of both of you."

My heart skipped a beat. "Well, I didn't mean to. I was just looking out for Fuzz."

"I know," she said, "but the problem is that Big Ted will interview everyone who was at your dinner, and he's going to find out that Fuzz and Tawny had an argument. When he does, he'll wonder why you didn't tell him about it."

I swallowed hard. It was starting to feel like I might have bungled this one. "What do I do now?"

Maddie put an arm around my shoulder. "Simple, Mom. Spill the beans to Big Ted, every last detail. It's the only way to clear the air and get you and Fuzz back in the good graces of the law."

# CHAPTER 4

The Beechtree police force poked around the lodge all morning. I tried to get Big Ted's attention to clear up my story about dinner, but his deputy waved me off and promised Big Ted would circle back later.

Frustrated, I retreated to Cabin 1. Tawny and George's cabins, Cabin 5 and Cabin 6, were off-limits and sealed with police tape. The business guy was in Cabin 2, leaving Cabin 3 and Cabin 4 vacant. At some point we'd have to completely renovate every cabin on the property, but for now, they were all cleaned and ready for guests.

Except for Cabin 1. Located near the parking lot, it provided an ideal spot for monitoring the comings and goings of the lodge. By moving it to the top of my to-do list, I could get Cabin 1 ready for the festival and keep an eye out for Big Ted at the same time.

A wave of musty air greeted me when I opened the door. Inside, the cabin's log walls desperately needed a good scrubbing, and a thin coat of dust covered the furniture. It was time to work some magic and bring this relic back to life.

After opening the windows to let some fresh air in, I

grabbed a bucket of soapy water and a soft-bristled brush. Then I began gently scrubbing the walls, removing layers of dirt. It was a slow process, but it felt satisfying to see the log walls' natural texture gradually reappear.

Next, I tackled the stone fireplace. The centerpiece of the living area, the fireplace showed ash and soot buildup from years of use. Gloves on, wire brush and dustpan in hand, I scraped away the grime, uncovering the gorgeous stonework beneath.

In the bathroom, I polished the dull tiles to a shine and replaced its worn towels with fluffy ones. I also replaced the bathmat with a plush rug, the kind that feels luxurious underfoot. As an added touch, I placed a tray of fragrant, eco-friendly hand soap and lotion near the sink.

Finally, it was time to bring it all together with some flourishes in the bedrooms and living room. I opened the boxes of supplies I'd ordered online and replaced threadbare sheets with buttery-soft linens. The blankets, fluffy and warm, draped over the beds, promising guests a night of rest and relaxation.

In the living room, I replaced worn-out quilts with soft, fleecy throws. I also added some pillows to create a cozy nook for reading or cuddling.

With the final touches in place, I stepped back to admire my work. For the first time in a long time, the cabin felt like a sanctuary instead of a museum.

Evie sauntered in as I was packing up my supplies. "This place cleans up pretty nice," she said.

"Right?" I looked around the cabin. "I'd book a weekend here."

"Same," Evie said, eyeing the new throw blankets. "Oh, by the way, Big Ted's finally gone. George, Betsy, and Wanda left too. Can you believe Big Ted didn't even let George retrieve his shaving kit before they sealed his cabin?"

"Big Ted left already?" I glanced at my smartwatch and saw that I'd worked straight through lunch—and straight through my chance to make things right with the local police chief. "I really needed to talk to him."

"I guess you'll just have to swing by the station later," Evie said. "Speaking of Big Ted, did he interrogate you too?"

"Uh, yeah. He cornered me and Maddie at Warbler's End. And he was kind of a jerk."

"Tell me about it," Evie scoffed. "Can you believe he asked me if I smoke weed? I guess he thinks all Black folks are potheads."

"That's outrageous!" I exclaimed.

Evie sighed and shrugged her shoulders. "What can you do?"

"Did Big Ted ask you about the dinner?" I asked casually, pretending to rearrange the pillows on the couch.

Evie nodded, bending down to snatch a stray piece of paper towel off the floor. "He was practically obsessed with it. Dinner was about the only thing he wanted to talk about."

That didn't sound good. If Big Ted was zeroing in on the dinner, he likely knew about Fuzz and Tawny's spat.

"And what did you tell him?" I pressed.

"Just the basics—who showed up, what they said, and when they took off," she replied, straightening up.

"So, did you mention Fuzz and Tawny's blow-up?" I probed.

Evie looked at me, slightly puzzled. "Of course, I did. Didn't you?"

"Well, not exactly," I confessed. "That's what I wanted to talk to him about. You know, changing my story."

"Changing your story?" Evie crossed her arms, waiting for me to elaborate.

I scratched my nose. "I might have left out the part about

Fuzz and Tawny's blow-up, I'll stop by the station later and smooth things over. Any updates from Fuzz?"

According to Evie, Fuzz hid out in his cabin until Big Ted summoned him and then took off after the interview ended. He sent Evie a text saying he and Charley were picking up something at the hardware store, but that had been a while ago.

"Have you heard from the guy in Cabin 2?" I asked.

"Not a peep. By the time Big Ted got around to interviewing him, the business guy was gone for the day. We're supposed to tell him to stop by the police station if we see him."

"When is he checking out?" I asked.

"He's paid up through Wednesday," Evie replied, "but he might stay Thursday night too."

I frowned. "Um, hold on . . ."

"Relax. Fuzz told him he has to leave first thing Friday because the cabins are all booked for the festival."

Friday was crunch time. We'd planned to avoid house-cleaning duties so we could focus on guest check-ins and last-minute festival preparations. Hopefully the business guy would leave on Thursday so we didn't have to turn over his room in the middle of Friday's chaos.

When I asked Evie about her plans for the rest of the day, she mentioned tackling the flowerbeds. They needed weeding, and she planned to work outdoors until dinner. Meanwhile, I planned to visit the cafe to discuss festival concessions with Wanda.

Evie wagged her finger. "And don't forget about Nora."

"Right, thanks for reminding me." Nora had completely slipped my mind. Why hadn't she shown up yet? She'd seemed so excited about the festival the last time I'd talked to her.

"Any chance you could call her when you get a minute?" I asked.

"Sure. I'll keep an eye on the lodge and give Nora a ring this afternoon. All right, last thing. Any cravings for dinner?" she asked.

Evie and I shared a cabin tucked between Tawny's cabin and Black Spruce Marsh. Although it was small, it had everything we needed: two cozy bedrooms, a decently equipped kitchen, a full bathroom, and a fireplace that kept us warm on chilly summer nights.

We loved our simple living arrangement. When we weren't working on the lodge, we usually spent our evenings burning a casserole or watching our favorite reality shows on the cabin's janky TV. Recently, we'd fallen out of our routine because I'd started spending more nights with Sam.

"About dinner," I began, my tone hesitant.

Evie connected the dots. "You're having dinner with Sam. Don't sweat it. If I were in your shoes, I'd do the same thing."

I smiled. "Thanks, Evie. We'll do dinner soon. By the way, don't wait up for me. It might be a sleepover."

Evie flashed a cheeky grin. "See you in the morning."

# CHAPTER 5

*W*ith Cabin 1 back in service, I headed to the Birdmobile, my trusty Subaru Forester parked in the family lot behind the lodge. Decorated with a mosaic of nature decals, she was fully outfitted for a day of hiking or birding. I liked to think of her as a rolling ode to Mother Nature.

The interior of the Birdmobile felt like a sauna, and streams of sweat rolled down my face as I blasted the AC. While I waited for cool air to filter through the vents, I sent Fuzz a quick text, asking him to call me ASAP. When there was no reply, I shifted the Birdmobile into gear and set off toward town.

Fuzz had been a homebody ever since Mom passed away. Evie and I routinely offered to keep an eye on things so he could go fishing or hang out at the Hop House with his buddies, but he always had an excuse. For some reason, he couldn't pry himself away from the place. Now, he was suddenly nowhere to be found.

To take my mind off Fuzz, I decided to play "I Spy." Although it felt a little juvenile, it used to be my favorite car game when I was a little girl, and I still associated it with Beechtree.

Right away, I spied the Knotty Pine Bookshop, with its squeaky wooden floors and old paper smell. Then I spied the Beechtree Bakery. I imagined the aroma of fresh-baked bread and pastries as I drove by.

A few doors down from the bakery, my much older eyes spied Sam's store, Abbott's Mercantile. The mercantile was a Beechtree fixture, complete with an aged facade and antique signage. When Sam's grandfather owned it, he mostly sold bulk goods to local businesses. Sam had expanded it into a general store and stocked it with everything from hardware and fishing gear to hand-crafted candles and touristy kitsch.

I resisted the urge to check in on Sam and continued down Main Street until I reached Wanda's Beary Good Cafe. The Beary Good was Beechtree's go-to eatery, serving a mix of classic and quirky meals that kept both tourists and locals coming back for more.

Inside, the lunch crowd had thinned, but the atmosphere remained lively. Decked out in tie-dye leggings and a bright red hairband, Wanda darted from table to table, greeting her patrons and keeping their glasses filled with iced tea.

"Joining us for lunch?" Wanda called out, guiding me to an open stool at the counter and placing a glass of iced tea in front of me. "Today's special is a grilled Caprese panini with creamy buffalo mozzarella and heirloom tomatoes. Picked the basil myself this morning."

My stomach growled. Wanda's sandwiches were legendary, but I had a lot to do before dinner with Sam. "As fantastic as that sounds, I'm just here to talk about the concession stand for the festival."

Wanda walked me through a tantalizing menu of sandwiches, sides, and desserts. The grilled portobello sandwich with goat cheese and pesto sounded divine. And there was no way I was leaving the festival without a slice of her famous chocolate cream pie.

With the concession stand sorted out, Wanda propped her elbows on the counter. "What a day, huh? The whole town's talking about Tawny," she said, her voice giddy. "Big Ted asked me a bunch of questions before I left your place, but he was tight-lipped about the details. So, what's the dealio?"

I'd naively hoped Tawny's death might fly under the radar for a few days—a dead body wasn't a good look for the festival or the lodge. But now that it was public knowledge, I could only imagine the wild stories swirling around town. The sooner the medical examiner released his report, the better.

"Big Ted's confident it was an accident," I said. "He thinks she probably fell into the marsh and drowned."

Wanda shook her head. "Life's unpredictable, isn't it?" Then lowering her voice, she added, "Between you and me, I wouldn't be surprised if someone knocked her off. Tawny ruffled a lot of feathers around here."

I'd heard rumors about Tawny's shady real estate dealings and dodgy mayoral maneuvers. Her reputation would undoubtedly provide even more grist for the rumor mill.

I thanked Wanda for organizing the concession stand and said my goodbyes. As I left the cafe, my phone vibrated in my pocket. I moved out of the doorway to make room for Wanda's customers and checked the screen, hoping to see Fuzz's number on the display.

It was Evie.

"Hey Evie, what's going on?"

"You won't believe what just happened," she blurted out. "Nora just told me someone phoned her last week and canceled her festival appearance."

It took a few seconds for my brain to process the news. "That doesn't make any sense. Who did she talk to?"

"No clue," Evie said. "Nora thought the caller might have been a woman, but the voice was muffled. So, who knows?"

I ignored the knot forming in my stomach and tried to stay calm. "Please tell me you set her straight. She's still coming to the festival, right?"

"It's a good news, bad news thing," she said. "The good news is that Nora can't wait to visit the lodge and talk about the bird species of the Adirondacks."

I breathed a short-lived sigh of relief. "And the bad news?"

"It's not happening this weekend because she's made other plans. On Saturday, Nora will be on a boat off Long Island, looking for gannets and storm petrels."

"What do we do now?" I asked, exasperated. Nora's cancellation was a major blow and I hoped Evie had a backup plan in mind.

"Nora was our headliner," she said. "People are going to be really disappointed if she's not there."

My sneakers slapped the concrete as I paced back and forth on the sidewalk. "But people have booked their travel and the vendors have invested time and money helping us get this thing off the ground. We can't just shut it down now."

"So, we soldier on," Evie said, her voice determined. "We'll figure something out."

"We both know who's behind this, right?"

Evie didn't miss a beat. "Tawny."

I sighed, rubbing my temple with my free hand. "From what I've heard, she's more than capable of pulling off a stunt like this."

"No doubt about it," Evie agreed. "This might sound cold, but now that she's out of the picture, maybe we can avoid any more curveballs."

As I walked to the Birdmobile, I had to admire Tawny's deviousness. Her argument with Fuzz showed that she had her own plans for the lodge. Canceling Nora was her attempt to sabotage the festival and ruin our efforts to turn the place around. If we couldn't figure out a way to make the festival happen without Nora, her plan might still work.

We needed a plan of our own, and we needed it fast.

# CHAPTER 6

*S*am and I settled into a corner booth at the Hop House and dug into slices of Hawaiian pizza piled high with juicy pineapple and crispy bacon. He took a swig from his hazy Hop House IPA. "Sounds like you had an eventful day."

"I'm not sure what was worse," I said, wiping pizza grease from my lips. "The part where I implicated Fuzz and me as co-conspirators in an imaginary murder, or the part where an evil genius ruined our festival."

"They're both pretty bad," Sam agreed. "I still don't understand why Tawny and Fuzz hate each other so much."

"Like I said last night, I don't know what Tawny and Fuzz were arguing about at dinner. It's no secret that Tawny and Fuzz have been butting heads about the lodge, though."

"What do you mean?" he asked.

I explained that when Tawny ran for mayor, she'd campaigned on a promise to bring Beechtree, kicking and screaming, into the twenty-first century. Since taking office, she'd worked with the zoning board to drive out the businesses she deemed eyesores. Based on the zoning board's recent actions, it seemed like the lodge was next on her list.

"Is that legit?" he asked. "The lodge's zoning has been in place for decades."

"Apparently, it's completely legal. Tawny's cronies on the zoning board can say the lodge's lack of occupancy demonstrates a change of use from business to residential. If that happens, Fuzz loses his certificate of occupancy, and the lodge is finished. Probably for good."

Sam furrowed his brow. "Hold on a sec. You said Tawny mentioned property value at dinner. That sounds like more than a zoning issue."

"Everyone knows Tawny only ran for mayor to benefit her and George's real estate agency. I don't know what she's up to, but I wouldn't be surprised if she'd found a way to profit off the businesses she forced out."

"Well, I've done business with Tawny a couple of times, and she always seemed professional to me," he said. "Just to be safe, you should probably tell Big Ted about the zoning thing."

"I tried to," I said, grabbing another slice of pizza. "I even stopped by the police station after I checked in with Wanda at the café, but Big Ted wasn't there. Annie said he was at the medical examiner's office in Malone."

Although her official title was receptionist, Annie Garza ran the show at Beechtree PD. While Big Ted stole the spotlight, Annie kept the gears of justice grinding smoothly. She was also an enthusiastic birder and longtime member of the Fly Girls. And she had promised to tip me off if she overheard anything about the investigation at the station. It was a risky gamble. Annie could get fired if she got caught, but that's what Fly Girls were about. Having each other's backs.

Over slices of pizza, Sam and I traded stories about growing up in Beechtree. Although he was seven years younger than me, I discovered that we counted some of the same people in our friend groups.

I also learned that he had a business degree from SUNY Plattsburgh. It was another thing we had in common. I'd received a biology degree from the SUNY School of Environmental Science and Forestry in Syracuse. As we polished off our remaining slices, we compared our college experiences. We both gave our schools high marks for providing a solid, affordable education—the SUNY system was a real godsend for families like ours.

"Did you ever think about moving back to Beechtree after college?" he asked.

I grinned. "Absolutely. In a perfect world, I would've returned to Beechtree the day I got my diploma and never looked back. But by that time, Kevin and I were engaged. He was finishing his final year of law school at Syracuse, and we were moving to Rochester so he could work at his dad's law firm. Coming back to Beechtree wasn't really on the table at the time."

"But maybe it's on the table now that you're divorced?"

Sam and I hadn't talked about our future yet, and I dreaded the conversation. I didn't want to hurt his feelings though, so I chose my words carefully.

"Like I said before, Evie and I are just visiting Beechtree to relax and enjoy a summer in the mountains. The problems at the lodge have complicated our plans, but once it's back on its feet, we're most likely headed back to Rochester."

"Fair enough," he said. "What's waiting for you in Rochester?"

That was a good question. Apart from a house and an ex-husband, there wasn't much anchoring me to the city. Thanks to a healthy divorce settlement, I had the financial freedom to live wherever I wanted to, at least for a while. But Beechtree? Although I loved the place, I didn't see myself making it my forever home. Beechtree felt more like a detour than a destination.

"Look, Sam, I really enjoy spending time with you. If I'm honest, I think we might have something special, but we've only dated for a few months. I'm here with you now. That counts for something, doesn't it?"

He forced a smile, but I could tell he was hiding his disappointment. "I suppose so," he said in a deflated tone. "For now."

Any traces of awkwardness between Sam and me disappeared when a fiery redhead with an athletic build breezed up to our table. "Hey, guys! How's date night going?"

Liliana Bloom was a force of nature. Though she had a reputation as a top-notch climber, I was more familiar with her birding skills. At just twenty-four, she had some of the sharpest birding ears I'd ever encountered. Her ability to identify species by sound alone was the stuff of legends in the Adirondack birding community.

Over the past year, Liliana and I had bonded through family events and our shared love of birding. Beyond her many talents, she had a heart of gold and showered Maddie with affection. In a lot of ways, Liliana was like a second daughter.

I finished my last bite of pizza and gestured at our empty plates. "The Hawaiian was delicious, like always. I heard you have a date night of your own tomorrow."

Liliana rolled her eyes as she piled our plates and silverware into a bus tub. "That's the plan, but you know how it is. One employee calls in sick and date night's toast." She glanced around the restaurant, looking for the busboy. "Any updates on Tawny?"

"Nothing yet," I said. "Annie said it might take a few days for the medical examiner's report to come in."

Liliana turned to Sam. "How about you, big guy? What are you up to?"

"Just trying to keep our girl here out of trouble," he said, winking at me.

Liliana burst into laughter. "That's no easy feat."

"I was hoping to run into you," I said. "Have you talked to Fuzz lately?"

Liliana deftly stacked plates in the tub. "Nope, not since this morning. Is everything okay?"

I gave a small shrug as I dumped my remaining silverware into the container. "I'm sure he's fine. It's just that he left the lodge right after he talked to Big Ted, and now he's not responding to my texts."

"Big Ted, huh? That guy's a trip," she muttered, wiping her hands on her apron.

I chuckled. "You're telling me."

"Hey, are you going to Fly Girls tomorrow?" Liliana asked.

The Fly Girls met at eight o'clock every Wednesday morning at the Hop House. Wednesdays were Wanda's day off at the cafe, and everyone preferred mornings because the birding was better. Some weeks we ventured into the field, and other weeks we stayed at the Hop House and talked about the latest birding news or planned upcoming excursions. Sometimes we even had a speaker.

"It's on my calendar," I lied. With everything going at the lodge, the Fly Girls meeting had slipped my mind.

"Awesome sauce," Liliana chirped. "By the way, your dinner is on me."

"Not a chance," Sam protested. "I already promised to pay. You don't want to make a liar out of me, do you?"

True to his word, Sam settled the bill, and we walked out into the night air. The sky was a blanket of stars, shining like diamonds against an inky canvas.

"Any interest in spending the night at the RV?" he asked.

"Maybe, but I have to swing by the lodge and talk to Fuzz before Fly Girls. If I stay, I'm setting a super-early alarm."

"Not a problem," he said. "In fact, let's make a bet. If I'm awake before your alarm goes off, you owe me our next pizza." His ploy for another date wasn't very subtle, but lucky for him, I was totally on board.

"You're on."

# CHAPTER 7

*S*am nudged me awake a good twenty minutes before the alarm went off. He couldn't resist gloating about winning our bet, leaving me on the hook for our next pizza night.

After a quick sink bath, I filled a travel mug with coffee and steered the Birdmobile toward the lodge.

Fuzz's truck sat parked outside his cabin, at the property's southern edge. I grew up in that cabin and seeing it always made me smile. As I rolled up the driveway, I remembered chasing fireflies through the field with Mom and building snow forts in the yard with Fuzz. I couldn't count the number of times I dozed off in the front porch hammock reading a Nancy Drew book.

I parked the Birdmobile next to Fuzz's truck and knocked on the cabin door. I didn't have to knock, but a little formality was a small price to pay if it prevented me from seeing Fuzz in his underwear.

When Fuzz didn't answer, I jumped back into the Bird-mobile and continued up the driveway to the lodge. Fuzz and Charley usually woke up at the crack of dawn and took a morning stroll around the property. If they stuck to their normal routine, they'd show up at the lodge soon, desperate for a cup of coffee and a bowl of kibble.

In the meantime, I decided to stop by my cabin for a quick shower. When I turned my key in the lock, the door didn't budge. The deadbolt. Evie must've forgotten I was out and flipped it out of habit. I gently rapped my knuckles on the cabin's wood door and waited.

A few minutes later, Evie appeared wearing a banana-colored bathrobe. She spoke in a soft voice. "Hey Honey, how's it going? Here's the thing . . . I had my own sleepover last night."

I was floored. Evie had been married a few times and occasionally dated back in Rochester, but she hadn't said anything about a boyfriend here in Beechtree. "Really?" I stammered. "Good for you, Evie. Who's the lucky guy?"

Evie motioned for me to lower my voice. "If you could give me an hour, I'd really appreciate it."

"No problem," I said, feeling a little awkward. "I guess I'll go over to the lodge office and check for new reservations. If you see Fuzz, can you let him know I'm looking for him?"

"Will do," Evie said, mouthing a silent "thank you" before closing the door.

As I turned toward the lodge, my mind was so preoccupied with Evie's mystery man that I almost missed the figure peering into the window of the cabin next door. It was Tawny's cabin, and my adrenaline surged.

"Excuse me, can I help you?" I tried to sound intimidating, but even I had to admit that it wasn't very convincing.

The man whirled around, startled. Tall and attractive, he wore khakis and a baby blue polo shirt. I didn't know who he was, but at least he didn't look like a serial killer.

"Hi there," he said. "Do you work here?"

"Sort of. My family owns this place."

"Your dad must be Fuzz, right? I met him the other night. I'm Rupert Lloyd." He reached for a handshake. When he noticed my confusion, he pointed to the row of cabins and added, "Cabin 2."

The business guy. I relaxed a little when I realized he wasn't a peeping Tom but a paying customer. "Honey Palmer. Nice to meet you."

"Sorry if I scared you," Rupert apologized. "I was just admiring the lake. The view is something else."

"You mean the lake inside that cabin?" I crossed my arms and raised an eyebrow.

Rupert's cheeks reddened. "I swear, I'm not up to anything shady. Just enjoying the scenery."

We both knew his explanation was totally bogus, but I let it slide. I had enough problems on my plate today.

"You know, you shouldn't be here. I don't know if you heard about the accident yesterday, but the police sealed off that cabin as a precaution."

Rupert's eyes widened. "I spent the entire day at Lake Placid. What happened? Is everyone all right?"

"Actually, no," I said. "A woman accidentally drowned in the marsh two nights ago."

Rupert's expression grew serious. "That's awful. I had no idea."

I explained that the police were still investigating the incident. "It seems like it was just a really sad accident," I said.

"Well, again, I'm sorry I startled you. I didn't mean to cause any trouble."

"It's fine. Just stay away from that cabin." As I walked away, I remembered something else. "Oh, by the way," I called back, "the Beechtree police chief wants you to stop by the station. He's interviewing everyone who was on the property at the time of the accident."

Rupert looked puzzled. "I'm not sure how I can help. I

was exhausted and hit the sack right after I checked in. Slept like a baby all night long."

"I understand, but you should tell the police everything you know. I'm sure they're just trying to get a better idea what happened." The irony of my own reluctance to share everything I knew with Big Ted wasn't lost on me.

Rupert nodded a bit too enthusiastically for my liking. "You bet. I'll swing by the station later today."

"Thanks. And remember, stay away from that cabin."

"Sure thing," he said, waving goodbye.

Rupert seemed fishy. He was clearly snooping around Tawny's cabin, and his sudden appearance at the lodge seemed a little strange too. Though I didn't trust him, he didn't strike me as dangerous. Smarmy, maybe. But not dangerous.

I unlocked the lodge office, started the coffeemaker, and logged into the reservation system while it brewed. My heart sank a little when I opened our email. No new reservations. Not even a trickle from third-party travel sites.

It was supposed to be the lodge's busiest season, but we were struggling to sell rooms. I reminded myself to stay positive. The festival could change everything. With luck, attendees would fall in love with the place, post photos on their Instagram accounts, and recommend it to everyone they knew. To tilt the odds in our favor, I made a mental note to talk up the lodge's discounts and packages on festival day.

I refilled my travel mug with coffee and powered down the computer. The next few days wouldn't be easy, but we'd make them count. Before we did anything else, we had to fill the Nora-shaped hole in the festival.

And I had an idea I couldn't wait to share with the Fly Girls at our morning meeting.

~

Fuzz and Charley were still missing when I left the lodge for the Fly Girls meeting. I arrived at the Hop House a few minutes early and sat in the Birdmobile to make a list of everything we still needed to do.

First on the list? Check the weather. If the forecast called for a soggy Saturday, we might have to round up more tents. After that, I needed to double-check Fuzz's old-school sound equipment and sort out the vendor tents.

I was in the middle of jotting down more tasks when my phone vibrated. Glancing at the screen, I saw it was Annie.

"Take a deep breath," she began, her voice low.

I tensed up, expecting the worst. "What's going on?"

"I don't have much time, so bear with me," she said. "Big Ted called everyone into work early today."

"Why?" I asked. The urgency in her voice really had me concerned.

"Remember when I mentioned Big Ted was in Malone yesterday?" Her voice dropped to a whisper. "He expedited the medical examiner's report, and he went to the ME's office himself to make sure it was a top priority."

"And?" I prodded, waiting for the other shoe to drop.

"Just so you know, he's not releasing any information to the public yet," Annie continued.

The suspense was getting on my nerves. "Just spit it out, Annie. What's going on?"

"The medical examiner's report came in overnight, and Tawny's death wasn't an accident."

"How is that possible?" I asked, dumbfounded.

"I'm not sure. I just wanted you to know before things start to spiral. Big Ted's in beast mode, and there's only one thing on his mind."

"What's that?" I asked, but I knew what she was going to say.

"Finding Tawny's killer."

# CHAPTER 8

*T*he Fly Girls took the news about Nora's cancellation pretty hard.

"There's no Nora?" Betsy asked, glossing over the news that some charlatan had canceled Nora's appearance to purposely tank the festival.

"Apparently not," I replied.

"Fantastic," Betsy grumbled. "Nora's talk was the only part of the festival I was excited about."

Wanda cast a sidelong glance at Betsy. "Am I the only one who thinks this whole thing is bizarre?"

"Bizarre doesn't scratch the surface, but we have to find a replacement for Nora." Evie tossed her notebook on the table. "The festival doesn't work without a keynote speaker."

"I agree with you there," Betsy said. "The problem is that you won't find a decent speaker on short notice. You want my advice? Cancel the festival. Or at least postpone it until you can sort everything out."

"We already decided that canceling the festival isn't an option," I insisted. "Vendors and attendees have made plans to be here, and we can't back out now. The festival is happening in three days, no matter what."

"Atta girl!" Liliana cheered. I could see why Maddie liked her so much. Liliana had a knack for making you feel good about yourself even when things looked grim.

"Any ideas?" Evie scanned the room for suggestions.

"I have one, but it's not a person. It's a group. And not just any group." I let the suspense build for a few seconds. "It's us."

I pitched my idea to feature the North Country Fly Girls as the main attraction of the festival. Although we were all experienced and passionate birders, we also had an important story to tell. We were a women-only birding club.

Groups like the Fly Girls were unique because they offered a supportive environment for women who love nature and birdwatching. Our club provided a space where female birders could connect and learn without feeling overshadowed or dismissed.

Women-only clubs also helped make outdoor environments safer for women. I'd recently read some alarming statistics about violence against women, and I was horrified to learn that 60 percent of female runners had experienced harassment outdoors. But it wasn't just runners. Nearly every Fly Girl could point to a time when they'd felt unsafe in nature.

The beauty of clubs like ours was that they provided women with a network of female companionship so they could safely enjoy outdoor environments.

"If we make the Fly Girls the main attraction, we can raise awareness about an issue we all really care about," I argued. "We might even inspire some festivalgoers to start their own women-only birding clubs."

Wanda jumped out of her chair. "I love it! Instead of just one speaker, a bunch of us can talk about our experiences with the Fly Girls and explain why we think women-only clubs are important."

"Maybe we could even educate attendees about conservation, and the role women play in protecting bird habitats and advocating for the environment," Liliana added.

Our excitement built as we brainstormed ideas. Wanda said she could turn the concession stand over to a helper for a while and lead a discussion about the challenges female birders face, the benefits of women-only birding clubs, and strategies for creating more inclusive birding communities. Liliana volunteered to lead a few women-only birding hikes on the day of the event, and Evie's brain slipped into overdrive as she ticked off plans to promote the festival's new theme on social media and other marketing channels.

The plan was falling into place. The Fly Girls were more than just a group of women who stared through binoculars. We were ready to take center stage and shine a spotlight on female birders.

My other piece of news dampened my enthusiasm about the new direction for the festival. I still had to tell the group about Tawny's cause of death—and that information could derail everything.

"These are all great ideas, and I'm thrilled about the direction we're headed with the festival," I said, interrupting the group's brainstorm. "But there's something else. Annie called me a little while ago with some disturbing news. The medical examiner's report on Tawny's death is in, and it turns out her death wasn't accidental after all." I winced as the words left my mouth.

Wanda leapt out of her chair again. "I knew it!"

"I'm confused," Evie said. "If Tawny's death wasn't an accident, what was it? Murder?"

"I guess so," I replied.

The group erupted with questions, and I did my best to

answer them. "Why does Big Ted think it was murder?" I don't know. "Does he have any suspects?" No idea. "What was the murder weapon?" Really?

"The one thing I do know is that Big Ted isn't releasing this information to the public yet. I expect the whole town will know about it before long, but we need to keep it quiet until it's official," I said, staring directly at Wanda. "If Big Ted finds out that we knew about the medical examiner's report before it's made public, it could put Annie's job in jeopardy."

Though I seriously questioned Wanda's ability to keep quiet, I was glad to hear everyone agreed with the need to exercise discretion, at least in theory.

"What does that mean for the festival?" Liliana asked. "Is Warblers' End off limits?"

It was a valid question. Big Ted could restrict access to the entire side of the marsh that bordered the lodge's property, including Warblers' End. Part of the area was already cordoned off with police tape.

"You've got bigger problems than that," Betsy interjected. "Who's going to show up for a festival smack in the middle of a crime scene? You don't have a choice now. You have to cancel it."

I bristled. "We're not canceling the festival. It's too late for that."

Surprisingly, Evie wasn't so quick to dismiss Betsy's concerns. "Betsy has a point. Negative publicity is a death knell for attendance, and if people start associating the lodge with a murder, it's gonna be a tough sell."

"So, you think we should pull the plug too?" I asked, raking my fingers through my hair in frustration.

"No way, but we need to take control of the narrative," Evie replied. "If people are worried, we can point out that the police are investigating and then talk about how a tragedy like this brings people together in a small town like

Beechtree. It's all about framing the conversation in a way that reassures people about their safety."

"I think Tawny's murder might actually help the festival," Wanda exclaimed, catching everyone off guard. "One of the festival's goals is to promote a sense of security for women in the outdoors, isn't it? Well, Tawny was outdoors when . . ."

This was getting ridiculous. "Let's stay focused. We can't ignore the reality that Tawny's murder undoubtedly complicates things." There was no denying the fact that a police investigation could destroy everything Evie, Fuzz, and I had worked toward. If the festival fizzled, we had zero chance of turning the lodge around.

Liliana's voice jolted me back into the conversation. "If you think about it, Tawny's murder only poses a threat to the festival if the murderer is still on the loose."

Evie leaned forward in her chair. "What do you mean?"

"If the cops nab the killer before the festival, we're in the clear," Liliana explained. "It's not ideal, but at least we can assure everyone the festival is safe, and the incident at Warblers' End was a one-time event. A fluke."

"Lots of luck counting on Beechtree PD to find the killer any time soon," Betsy grumbled. "Big Ted's not known for his speediness, you know. It took him a week to question the Hodgson kids about vandalizing my flowerpots, and I had their faces on my doorbell camera."

"Maybe we could give Big Ted a hand," Evie suggested, a mischievous glint in her eye. It was a look I knew well—and it usually meant she was about to recruit me for another half-baked scheme. "What if we did some investigating ourselves?"

"I'm not sure that's a good idea. Big Ted won't tolerate us messing around with his murder investigation." He'd already warned Maddie to stay clear of the investigation, and she was an actual law enforcement officer. I could only imagine how he'd react to a group of bird-loving tree huggers getting in his way.

"Then we won't tell him about our investigation," Liliana said. "We won't do anything dangerous, but we'll steer clear of Big Ted. There's no harm in keeping our eyes and ears open, is there?"

"No, there isn't," Wanda answered, her voice filled with conviction. "You'd be amazed what I overhear at the cafe. If Big Ted planted himself at the Beary Good, he'd probably crack the case by lunchtime."

"I'll see what I can turn up at the Hop House. People tend to get talkative after a few beers," Liliana added.

"Annie's already eavesdropping at the police department, and if you can get Sam on board at the mercantile, we'd have most of Beechtree covered," Evie said. "What do we have to lose, Honey? It's worth a shot, don't you think?"

I harbored serious concerns about the countless ways Evie's plan could go sideways, but I couldn't argue with the group's logic. If we were careful and stayed in our lane, maybe we could uncover information that would help the police solve Tawny's murder. I'd rather tell attendees the case was closed than warn them to watch their backs.

"You know what? I'm in. Let's give it a shot," I said.

Wanda's eyes sparkled with excitement. "This is so awesome—a birding festival and a real-life murder mystery in the same week!" As she spoke, her salt-and-pepper curls bounced up and down, and her freckled cheeks took on a rosy hue.

"Control yourself, Wanda," Evie said. "We have a lot of work to do over the next few days. Let's roll up our sleeves and get started."

"And let's stay in touch," I said. "We'll use the Fly Girls text thread to communicate with each other about the festival and share anything we uncover about Tawny's murder."

It was a long shot, but sometimes the craziest ideas panned out. With the Fly Girls committed to the festival and quietly gathering intel for Big Ted, at least we had a chance to get things back on track.

# CHAPTER 9

After the Fly Girls' meeting, I headed to the lodge to finally track down Fuzz and learn more about his conversation with Tawny. As I pulled into the lodge's driveway, Maddie was leaving in her park service SUV. I shifted the Birdmobile into reverse and pulled alongside her, rolling down my window.

"What are you doing here? I thought you had to work today," I asked.

"I'm off to patrol Mount Baker right now, but I'm glad I bumped into you," she said.

It still felt strange seeing Maddie dressed in her ranger uniform. She had always loved nature, but I never imagined she would wind up in a career that required her to wear a duty belt and sidearm. Even though I appreciated her commitment to conservation, the law enforcement part of her job gave me the jitters.

I squinted to shield my eyes from the mid-morning sun. "Did Liliana fill you in?" I asked.

"She called me, but I'd already heard about the coroner's report," Maddie answered matter-of-factly. "Big Ted rang up

50

my supervisor at the crack of dawn and told her that the lodge is neck-deep in a murder investigation. And, of course, he trotted out that same old 'this town's not big enough for both of us' routine."

"What did your boss say?" I asked, chewing on my lip.

Maddie shrugged. "She's dealt with Big Ted before, so she wasn't surprised. Told me to keep my nose out of his investigation, though."

The idea of Big Ted making problems for Maddie at work bothered me, but her involvement in our undercover sleuthing would only invite more problems.

"Big Ted's got it under control," I assured her. "Let's just give him room to work."

"Don't bother, Mom. Liliana filled me in on the Fly Girls' investigation." When I didn't immediately respond, she added, "Relax, I'm going to steer clear of it."

"Great, then we're on the same page. Now, before you go, I have a forest ranger question," I said, feeling like a total hypocrite.

She chuckled. "What do you want to know?"

Resting my arm on the Birdmobile's door, I leaned toward her. "The medical examiner said Tawny's drowning wasn't accidental. How do they know that? Are there any signs that a drowning isn't just a mishap?"

Maddie explained that determining foul play in a drowning scenario was tricky, but not impossible. Things like broken nails or bruising might point to a struggle. Or if there were signs of restraint—like rope burns or handcuff marks—it could indicate the death was intentional. The medical examiner would also sift through the victim's clothing for clues.

"Did you pick that up at ranger school or from one of your podcasts?" I asked.

She flashed an impish grin. "A little of both."

"Well, wherever you picked it up, I'm impressed. I didn't see any bruises or scratches on Tawny's body, though. Did you?"

She shook her head. "That's not unusual. Scratches and other marks are easy to miss in the field. But I've been thinking about something else we saw at Warblers' End."

"I'm all ears," I said, "but then you have to promise to stay out of the investigation."

She raised her hand in a mock salute. "Scout's honor. Now, do you remember Tawny's nightgown?"

I nodded. "Sure, it was white with lace around the hem, and it was wet."

"How was her body positioned?" Maddie pressed.

"Face down, her head submerged in the marsh," I said, the image fresh in my mind.

"And where was the rest of her body?" she continued.

"On the shore." I suddenly realized what Maddie was getting at.

"Her nightgown was on the shore, and it was wet, which means at some point her entire body was in the water. If it was an accidental drowning, we would have probably found her body entirely in the water, not half in and half out," Maddie explained.

"Maybe there was a struggle," I reasoned, "and either the struggle moved back to land or the killer drowned her in the marsh then dragged her body out of the water after she was dead."

"You got it," she said. "Still, it's not concrete proof, so the medical examiner must have found something else that caused him to rule her death a homicide."

"Thanks, Maddie, this is helpful. Starting now, there's a firewall between you and the investigation."

"Absolutely," she said, but I knew keeping her out of it wouldn't be easy. "By the way, Fuzz is waiting for you at the lodge," she said. Then she gave a quick wave, shifted the SUV into gear, and drove off.

I felt oddly upbeat. It wasn't even ten o'clock yet and we'd already mapped out new plans for the festival, pieced together some theories about how Tawny might have died, and located Fuzz.

At the lodge, I found Charley prancing around the lawn, his nose deep in the hydrangeas that Evie and I had planted earlier in the season. The flowers, bursting in shades of pink and purple, offset the lodge's rustic brown timbers in a way that looked almost professional. While I admired the land-scaping, Charley lifted his leg and took aim at the hydrangea nearest the entrance.

"Charley!" I yelled, scowling. "Back off the hydrangeas!"

He glanced my way, tail wagging, and continued to sniff the rest of the flowers. As I approached to give him a pat, Fuzz appeared from around the corner of the building.

"Hey there, kiddo."

"Where have you been?" I was relieved to see him, but I was still annoyed that he'd ghosted me the day before.

Fuzz sprawled out on a porch step. "Let's see," he said. "This morning, Charley and I went for a walk. Then we came back to the lodge, and I had a few cups of coffee. After that, the caffeine kicked in and I had my morning constitutional, which was kind of unusual today because . . ."

"All right, spare me the details," I interrupted. "You know that's not what I meant. Where were you all day yesterday, and why didn't you answer my texts?"

"Didn't Evie tell you? I needed a part for the John Deere, and Charley and I had to drive all the way to Lake Placid to get it. Then we drove around for a while. I needed to clear my head."

I appreciated the need for a mental breather, but there was something else I had to know.

"Okay, then what did Tawny say that made you blow up at dinner?" I asked, shifting gears.

Fuzz tensed up. "Does it matter?"

I walked over and sat beside him on the steps. "I think it does. I'm trying to piece together what happened."

His shoulders slumped. "Fine. Tawny brought up the zoning issue again when you and Evie went to the kitchen to get dessert. Then she pressured me to sell her the lodge."

"Sell the lodge?" My heart raced. "Why would you do that? We're working so hard to turn it around."

"Exactly my point," Fuzz said, visibly frustrated. "But she said it was just a matter of time before the lodge went under, and I should just make it easier on both of us and sell it to her now. That was the last straw for me. I lost it."

Now that I knew what it was about, I didn't blame Fuzz for losing his cool at dinner. The thought of someone like Tawny owning the lodge nauseated me.

"Did you tell Big Ted about the zoning board and Tawny's sudden interest in the lodge?" I asked.

He scratched his beard. "Nah. To be honest, I didn't think it was any of his business."

"I didn't mention the argument to Big Ted either," I confessed. "He knows something happened between you and Tawny, though. I left a message at the police station telling him I want to update my statement. You should do the same thing as soon as you can."

"You'll have a chance to clear things up with Big Ted sooner than you think," Fuzz said. "He just called the lodge's landline and he's bringing over a state police detective to go through George's and Tawny's cabins this afternoon. Probably just tying up loose ends."

Loose ends? It occurred to me that Fuzz was missing an important piece of information. "You don't know, do you?" I asked.

54

"Know what?" He looked genuinely puzzled.

"A few hours ago, Annie Garza told me the medical examiner ruled Tawny's death a homicide. Big Ted isn't tying up loose ends, he's conducting a murder investigation. That's why the state police are involved."

"A murder investigation, huh?" I watched, amazed, as he pulled out a Swiss army knife and began picking his teeth with the toothpick. "Sounds serious."

"It is serious!" I explained that Tawny's interest in the lodge gave him a motive for her murder. Throw in the fact that we had both neglected to mention the argument, and Big Ted could easily point the finger at the two of us as the prime suspect and his accomplice.

"Are you telling me that Big Ted thinks I killed Tawny? And you helped me cover it up?" Fuzz guffawed. "I've heard some whoppers in my time, but that one takes the cake."

He still wasn't grasping the seriousness of the situation. "This isn't a joke, Fuzz. We could be in real trouble."

"I know, I know," he said, still laughing. "Kiddo, don't worry about Big Ted. I didn't lay a finger on Tawny. He'll figure that out soon enough."

"I hope you're right, but Big Ted doesn't strike me as the kind of guy who lets facts get in the way of closing a case."

"Point taken," he agreed. "You know who Big Ted should really investigate? That guy in Cabin 2."

"You mean Rupert? Why do you say that?"

Fuzz relayed a conversation he had with Rupert when he checked in. Rupert said he was a heavy equipment salesman, in town to finalize a deal with a local construction company. Yet when Fuzz tried to talk to him about machinery, it was obvious Rupert didn't know the first thing about the equipment he claimed to sell. Fuzz said it was like talking to a fish about the joys of riding a bicycle.

"He didn't even know the difference between a bulldozer and a backhoe!" he exclaimed.

"Okay, that's weird," I conceded. "But why would he kill Tawny?"

He shrugged. "Beats me, but we should keep an eye on him."

The thought of hosting a possible murderer at the lodge made my skin crawl. On the other hand, we finally had a suspect who wasn't a family member.

Maybe things were starting to look up after all.

# CHAPTER 10

*I* found Evie hunkered down in the lodge's office, bright orange headphones covering her ears. She was tapping away at her keyboard, no doubt absorbed in the work of crafting emails and press releases for the festival's new theme. Not wanting to disturb her, I quietly slipped past the office, made my way to the great room, and sank into a couch near the fireplace.

The trill of a chipping sparrow drifted through an open window, and in the distance, I could hear Fuzz fire up the lawnmower. Shafts of sunlight streamed across the room, casting warm, dappled patterns on the hardwood floor and rustic furniture. Under different circumstances, I might have been inspired to meditate.

Instead, I grabbed a piece of paper from the reception desk, fully intending to map out a new event schedule for the festival. After several false starts, I moved the idea of a schedule revamp to the back burner, and started jotting down what we did and didn't know about Tawny's death.

In the "know" column, we knew Tawny died in or near the marsh at Warblers' End. Since the medical examiner had ruled out accidental causes, she must have gone to Warblers' End either on purpose or by force. We also knew that Tawny had plans to acquire the lodge. Combined with the argument at dinner, it painted a big target on Fuzz's back. Motive aside, I knew that Fuzz didn't kill Tawny. I added that one to the "know" column in the notebook.

Finally, there was Rupert. I knew he'd lied to me about snooping around Tawny's cabin, and I was pretty sure he'd lied to Fuzz about his reason for being in Beechtree. But we didn't know why he was really in town or if he even knew the Walters.

The "don't know" side of the list was a lot longer. We didn't know the reason why Tawny went to Warblers' End or who she met there. We also didn't know why she'd suddenly seemed so interested in the lodge or what she'd planned to do with it.

I didn't know the identity of Evie's mystery guest, either. Although it probably wasn't related to Tawny's death, I'd been mulling that one over for a while, so I added it to the list.

Getting back to the investigation, we didn't know who killed Tawny (obviously), and we didn't know who might have wanted to kill her, either. In fact, we didn't even know why the medical examiner had ruled her death a homicide.

I had too many questions about Big Ted to list. But I hoped we could move at least some of the "don't knows" about Tawny to the "know" column before he showed up with the state police.

I knew just the person for the job.

I FIRED off a text to Annie to see if she was free for lunch. Luckily she was available, but under the circumstances, she didn't think it was a good idea for us to be seen together in town or at the lodge. I couldn't argue with her there, so we decided to meet at Sam's RV.

Next, I gave Sam a quick call to fill him in on the Fly Girls' investigation and ask him to stay alert for any Tawny-related intel at the mercantile. He was happy to loan us the RV, and we made plans to have dinner together later. With the logistics in place, I made some sandwiches, gathered Evie, and set off for Sam's camper.

Annie bustled into the RV as Evie and I were setting out paper plates. A Latina in her early twenties, she wore jeans and a trendy blouse that highlighted her long hair. As usual, a backpack sat snugly over her shoulders, a carry-all for her yarn and knitting supplies.

"I don't have much time so let's skip the small talk, okay?" Annie dropped onto a cushioned bench in the dinette. I passed her a turkey sandwich and an orange seltzer as she gave us an update on Big Ted's investigation.

"First things first," Annie said. "Big Ted called in the cavalry, and they're heading to the lodge in about an hour."

I handed Evie her sandwich, then placed the last one in front of my place at the dinette's table. "Yeah, I know. Big Ted called Fuzz this morning to tell him that he's bringing a state police detective by the lodge to search Tawny's room."

"And a forensics team," Annie added, taking a bite of her sandwich.

"They're not gonna trash the place, are they?" Evie asked "Because that would really steam my beans. We've already booked Tawny's cabin for the weekend."

"No worries," Annie reassured her. "You might have to use some dish soap to remove the fingerprint dust, but no big deal, right?"

Annie went on to say that the medical examiner's report mentioned bruising on the back of Tawny's neck, suggesting someone had held her head underwater as she drowned. She pointed out that we probably didn't see the bruising at the scene because Tawny's shoulder-length hair concealed it.

Annie also said that the medical examiner's report noted that Tawny's nightgown was damp, and her blood alcohol content was 0.09 percent. Although Tawny's BAC made her legally drunk, she would have remained fully aware of her surroundings. Based on her body temperature and the temperature of the marsh water, the medical examiner estimated that she died in the early morning hours. The exact time of death was hard to pin down, but it was probably after midnight.

"Now the big question," Evie said. "Who's on Big Ted's list of suspects?"

"I don't have much information about that," Annie replied. "Big Ted is playing his cards close to his chest when it comes to suspects. Apart from the interviews he's already conducted at the lodge, he plans to talk to some folks in town later today. For now, he's focused on the lodge."

I didn't like the sound of that at all. The fact that Tawny's murder happened where we lived and worked was one thing, but Big Ted's focus on the lodge—and by extension, my family—was another thing entirely.

"We still have more questions than answers," Evie said, her voice full of frustration. "It's like we're stumbling around in the dark here."

I couldn't disagree. "Thanks for the info, Annie. We really appreciate it."

Annie smiled at us. "No problem. Oh, and George might swing by the lodge later today too. Big Ted told him he can retrieve his and Tawny's stuff after the state police are done searching their cabins."

With that, Annie said goodbye and headed back to the station. Before she left, I thanked her again for the information, and she agreed to contact me if there were any more developments in the case.

Evie and I had time to spare, so we hung back at the RV to finish our sandwiches. Sam was a stickler for cleanliness, and it showed. Despite the camper's small footprint, each item had its own dedicated space. The countertops gleamed, and the stainless-steel appliances glowed. Even the chairs looked like they had just rolled off the assembly line. Although I teased him about his obsession with cleanliness, the guy had a knack for transforming ordinary rooms into inviting spaces.

"I had no idea Sam was such a neat freak," Evie said as her eyes roamed around the RV. "I wish my guy cared about a spotless sink."

I couldn't resist. "Speaking of your guy . . . any chance you might give me a hint about who he is?"

Evie casually sipped her seltzer. "Nope, I'm not spilling any tea today. Besides, I'm not even sure how serious we are."

"But it must be kind of serious, right?" I knew Evie. If I pushed hard enough, she'd let something slip.

Evie put on her best poker face. "Time will tell. Let's talk about something else. What's your take on what Annie said?" she asked, clumsily changing the subject.

"Honestly? I think we're in a tough spot, especially Fuzz."

She wrinkled her eyebrows. "What makes you say that?"

"Well, it's kind obvious, isn't it?" I asked, slurping seltzer. "Big Ted only questioned people who were at the lodge, and he knows about the argument at dinner. I'll bet he's not talking about suspects because he already has someone in mind. Fuzz."

Evie laughed out loud. "Fuzz is a lot of things, but he's no killer. And he didn't have anything to do with Tawny's death. I'm positive about that."

"You know, Fuzz had a similar reaction when I told him

61

that he might be a suspect. He thought it was hilarious. Am I missing something?"

Evie shook her head. "You're not missing anything. It's just that Fuzz isn't the kind of person who could harm a fly, let alone another human being."

"You and I know that, but I'm not sure Big Ted's convinced," I countered.

"Believe me," Evie said, "Fuzz will come out of this smelling like a rose. He always does. Let's just focus on the festival and let Big Ted and the Fly Girls do their thing."

"You make it sound so easy."

"Easy peasy," Evie answered.

# CHAPTER 11

*F*uzz pretended to prune azaleas when Big Ted's entourage rolled into the lodge parking lot, leaving me to play hostess.

"This is Detective Childress," Big Ted said, introducing a woman in a crisp navy pant suit, "and these are her associates." He gestured vaguely at three figures decked out in hazmat suits.

Childress looked the part. Tall and slender, she wore her sandy hair tied back in a tight bun. The no-nonsense expression on her face spoke volumes, and her badge gleamed on her belt. When she shook my hand, her grip was so firm that it nearly popped my shoulder out of its socket.

Introductions over, I led the group across the parking lot to the cabins. Big Ted peeled away the police seals from the Walters' cabins and instructed me to unlock the doors as the forensics team started unpacking their gear. Then he waved me away, promising to let me know if they needed anything else.

"Actually, I'd like her to stick around in case I have any

questions," Childress said, stopping Big Ted in his tracks. "Is that all right with you, Ms. Palmer?"

"It's Honey," I said, "and of course, I'm happy to help however I can."

While the forensics team scoured George's cabin for evidence, Childress, Big Ted, and I explored Tawny's rooms. The living room was immaculate. A set of keys—presumably Tawny's—sat on the coffee table. The kitchenette also looked pristine, exactly the way I'd left it when I cleaned the cabin the previous weekend.

In the master bedroom, the bed was still made, the curtains were shut, and Tawny's empty suitcase rested on the luggage rack. The outfit she'd worn to dinner hung haphazardly on hangers in the closet.

Childress looked around. "No one cleaned the cabin since the victim checked in?"

"That's right," I said. "Tawny arrived about an hour before dinner, and Big Ted sealed up her cabin right after we found her."

Pressing on, she yanked open a dresser drawer and surveyed its contents. "No one else entered this room after the victim got here?"

"Not as far as I know," I affirmed.

"Interesting," she mumbled, without explanation.

Her comment piqued Big Ted's curiosity. "What's on your mind, detective?"

Childress gave Big Ted a look that could cut steel. Her expression made it clear that she had no intention of answering his questions anytime soon. Watching her put him in his place without a word was incredibly satisfying.

In the bathroom, she dug through Tawny's massive makeup case. I loved a good lipstick as much as the next girl, but seriously, how could one woman use even half of that stuff? Setting the makeup case aside, Childress rifled through the vanity drawers and inspected the trash bin by the sink. In the meantime, Big Ted started his own investigation of the cosmetics case.

While he worked to decipher the purpose of a beauty blender, Childress fished a crumpled piece of paper from the trash bin and smoothed it out on the bedroom desk. "This is a map of the property, isn't it?" she asked, holding it up for Big Ted to see.

He leaned in for a closer look. "Affirmative. There's a big red 'X' on Warblers' End where we found the body."

"There are also some numbers scribbled here," she said, motioning to a spot on the map. Then she passed it to me and asked, "What's your take, Honey?"

I immediately recognized it as the map we give guests when they check in. Someone had circled the places that offered the most scenic views, including Warblers' End. The numerals "1.35" were inked in blue at the top left corner.

"We give these to guests," I explained. "The 'X' on Warblers' End seems pretty clear, but the numbers? No clue."

"I know what they are," Big Ted chimed in. "It's a time: 1:35 a.m. That's when the killer told the victim to meet them at Warblers' End."

Childress shot him a skeptical look. "The period between the one and the three doesn't look like a time notation. If it's a time, it should be a colon."

"It's also oddly specific," I added. She raised an eyebrow, inviting me to continue. "I mean, who schedules a meeting for 1:35? Why not 1:30 or 1:45?"

"Maybe, but I'm not ruling out the theory that it's a time," he grudgingly conceded.

Childress finished her investigation of Tawny's cabin and we moved on to George's rooms. Despite a thorough search, she didn't turn up anything noteworthy, at least as far as I could tell.

As she continued sifting through George's things, I pulled Big Ted aside to tell him about Tawny and Fuzz's argument at dinner as well as the zoning stuff. Although he jotted down information about the zoning problem, he didn't seem surprised by my account of the argument. His reaction—or lack of it—confirmed my hunch that he already knew about the tension between Fuzz and Tawny.

As the forensics team packed up their equipment, Childress gave me the rundown. Except for the map, nothing looked out of the ordinary. The team still needed to analyze the fingerprints and other evidence they had gathered, but we were free to clean the rooms.

"Did you find the victim's cell phone at the scene?" she asked Big Ted.

He shook his head. "Negative. There was no phone with the body."

"That's weird," she remarked. "Tawny's cabin was sealed off. All her belongings should either have been in the cabin or on her body, but there was no cell phone at either location."

"I was thinking the exact same thing," Big Ted said.

Childress rolled her eyes. "I'm sure you were, Chief." I was really starting to like her.

She handed me her card as we walked back to the parking lot. "Good luck with your festival, Honey. I love the women-birders theme."

"Where did you hear about that? We only decided on the new theme a few hours ago."

"My birding group posted it on Facebook. Wouldn't miss it for the world," she said. Then she lowered the top of her blouse a few inches, just enough to reveal a chickadee tattoo on her upper chest.

Of course Childress was a birder. The cool kids usually were.

~

As CHILDRESS and Big Ted drove away, I noticed George's gray Lexus in the parking lot. That was fast—he must have zoomed over the second Big Ted gave him the go-ahead to pick up his and Tawny's stuff.

From my vantage point, the Lexus appeared empty, and George was nowhere to be found. As I turned to go back inside the lodge, he stepped out of Rupert's cabin, with Rupert close behind.

The pair were locked in a heated exchange. George's hands gestured wildly as he spoke while Rupert played defense. I couldn't make out what they were saying, but their conversation didn't seem very friendly.

It ended with George stabbing a finger in Rupert's chest, then storming off in the direction of the lodge. George's scowl quickly morphed into a smile when he noticed me watching them. He acted like everything was fine, but it was apparent the argument with Rupert had shaken him up.

"Is everything okay?" I asked.

George's eyes darted around the parking lot before meeting mine. "Yeah, everything's fine," he said. "I was just talking with one of your guests."

"I didn't realize you knew Mr. Lloyd. Are you two friends?" I asked.

George hesitated. "We just met today," he said finally, "but he seems like a decent guy. Anyway, I'm just here to grab our things. I'll get out of your way in a few minutes."

I walked George to the cabins and offered to help him pack up Tawny's belongings, but he politely asked me to wait outside. Several minutes later, he emerged from Tawny's cabin, clutching her suitcase and purse.

"All set?" I asked.

He nodded, his eyes fixed on the ground. "It's like a bad dream. Knowing Tawny was murdered makes everything a little harder."

I felt bad for the guy, but it didn't stop me from gently probing for information. "Do you have any idea who might have wanted to hurt Tawny? Did she have any enemies?"

"Tawny was a savvy businesswoman," he said, "but the real estate industry is ruthless. It's possible a disgruntled client or even a competitor was behind this."

I shared what I knew about the police investigation, then immediately regretted mentioning the map. Childress probably wouldn't want me spreading that piece of information around town. In any case, George speculated the map might be related to Tawny's plans for the lodge.

"Have you happened to see Tawny's cell phone lately?" I asked, changing the subject.

George thought for a moment. "Now that you mention it, no, I haven't seen it. Why?"

"The police didn't find it in her cabin or at Warblers' End."

George looked confused. "You mean it's missing?"

"Apparently," I replied. "The strange thing is Big Ted sealed her cabin right after we found her. No one went in there until today, which means she might've had the phone with her at Warblers' End."

As George loaded Tawny's suitcase into the trunk, he seemed eager to set the record straight about the things Tawny said at dinner. "I have no idea what Tawny was talking about when she mentioned her plans for the lodge. I don't want you to think I'm scheming to buy the lodge or something."

"I appreciate the honesty," I replied, "and I really am sorry about Tawny. If you need anything, just say the word."

As I watched George's Lexus drive away, I was sure he was hiding something. But for now, all I could do was keep my eyes and ears open and hope the truth would eventually come out.

# CHAPTER 12

By late afternoon, I'd finally turned my attention back to the festival. With just two days to go, Evie had plugged away at festival preparations while I dealt with the police and played junior detective. She probably thought she'd gotten the better end of the deal, but I didn't want her to feel like I was taking her hard work for granted.

She was in the great room with Betsy. George Clinton's "Atomic Dog" blasted from the lodge's sound system as the pair stenciled signage and grooved to the beat of eighties funk. When she saw me, Evie hustled into the office to turn down the volume, then hit me with a barrage of questions.

"Come on, spit it out. What happened with Big Ted?" Evie asked.

Sinking into one of the great room's comfy chairs, I shared that George had picked up his and Tawny's things. Then I provided a recap of Childress' search, this time leaving out the part about the map. I'd already said too much about the map to George. I would obviously tell Evie about it later, but I didn't want to bring Betsy or anyone else into the loop until I was sure it wouldn't interfere with the police investigation.

"That's all you found?" Betsy asked. "Sounds like a whole lot of nothing to me."

Betsy's relentless negativity might have been amusing if it wasn't so irritating. "Let's give the forensics team some time to go through the evidence," I said. "But here's an interesting tidbit—Tawny's cell phone is missing. Do either of you remember seeing it?"

Betsy shook her head. "I don't think she had one. I didn't see her with a cell phone at dinner, that's for sure."

"You're wrong," Evie corrected her. "I'm positive Tawny brought a cell phone to dinner. It was in a pink case, and it had a huge screen. I saw her messing around with it a bunch of times."

"So, we know that Tawny's cell phone disappeared some-time between dinner and when we found her at Warblers' End the next morning," I said. "It's not much, but it might be useful. I'll let Childress know that Tawny had her cell phone the last time we saw her."

Standing to my feet, I let my eyes roam over the array of signs scattered throughout the room. "What have the two of you been up to?"

Evie's eyes shone as she led me around the room, revealing the handmade signs she and Betsy had created. Though the last-minute theme change made professional signage impossible, Evie had risen to the occasion. Her concept was simple but effective: a series of placards featuring women who had made significant contributions to the fields of ornithology and conservation.

Looking around the room, I recognized several of my heroes. There was Phoebe Snetsinger, the first birder to observe more than 8,000 species in her lifetime. Rosalie Edge was also there, credited with establishing the world's first sanctuary for birds of prey at Pennsylvania's Hawk Mountain. And of course, Rachel Carson. Her groundbreaking book, "Silent Spring," exposed the devastating effects of DDT on birds and other wildlife in the 1960s.

Each placard included a photo of the woman, along with a concise biography and a list of their achievements. The display served as a visual tribute, a "who's who" of women who had made their mark on the world of birding.

Their attention to detail also extended to the functional signage for the event. Brightly colored signs would guide guests through the venue, while banners would advertise the names of vendors and sponsors. Ever the marketer, Evie had maintained a unified style using easy-to-read fonts and colors that matched the lodge's new branding.

"These signs are phenomenal!" I exclaimed. "How did you pull this together so fast?"

Evie brushed it off, as if all the work she had done was no big deal. After brainstorming a list of women to spotlight, she had hunted down images online, penned some quick bios, and slapped everything onto the placards. When Betsy showed up, the two of them made quick work of it.

"I noticed that the Fly Girls text thread has been awfully quiet, so I meandered over to see what's up," Betsy said. The house she inherited from her parents bordered the lodge to the south, and a path through the woods connected the two properties. When we were kids, Betsy and I used that path constantly, going back and forth between our houses. These days, she took advantage of it to check in on Fuzz and wander around the lodge's property. A little too frequently for Fuzz's taste.

"I know you don't want to hear it," Betsy continued, "but you should cancel the festival. The list of people who wanted Tawny out of the picture is a mile long, and I don't think Big Ted is going to find her killer anytime soon."

Betsy's constant calls to cancel the festival were wearing thin. "That train has already left the station," I said. "One way or another, the festival is happening this weekend. Besides, we wouldn't want to deprive people of seeing all these amazing signs you made, would we?"

Betsy didn't push it any further. With the signage project done, she headed home to feed her tabby cat, Mr. Whiskers. Now that it was just Evie and me, I filled her in on the map Childress had discovered in Tawny's cabin.

"Any thoughts about what we do next?" I asked.

"We still have a ton of work to do before the festival, but I think we've earned a breather," Evie said, stacking the signs in a corner.

"Oh, you have no idea how glad I am to hear that," I said, relieved. "I'm wiped out."

Evie had that look in her eye again. "I've got just the thing. Follow me."

$\sim$

TEN MINUTES LATER, I found myself sitting next to Evie in the lodge's lakeside gazebo. I had binoculars in one hand and a glass of Chardonnay in the other. We sat there, quietly soaking in the view of Beechtree Lake and the various birds that called our little piece of heaven home.

Among the Canada geese and mallards, a pair of double-crested cormorants caught our attention. Their glossy black feathers and hooked beaks were a dead giveaway, and we watched as they gracefully dove for fish. When they popped back up, they unfurled their wings, showing off an impressive wingspan of several feet.

Next up, a smaller, more compact bird glided past us. We instantly recognized it as a pied-billed grebe thanks to its unique bill—short, white, and marked with a vertical black stripe. White rump feathers accented the grebe's soft, brown plumage, a detail that was easy to miss at a glance.

"Penny for your thoughts," Evie said, breaking the silence.

"You can probably guess what's on my mind. The festival, the investigation, Fuzz. Pick one."

Evie's eyes stayed glued to the grebe. "Never a dull moment around here, is there?" I could hear the exhaustion in her voice. The Tawny situation was taking a toll on all of us.

"Do you regret coming to Beechtree?" I asked her. While I was glad to have Evie around, I knew she hadn't planned to spend the summer cleaning guest rooms and making signs.

"Not for a second. I've kind of fallen in love with the place. It's gorgeous here, and our little adventures have only made it more interesting." She pointed at the grebe. "Look at this! I'm seeing nature up close, and I couldn't ask for a better person to share it with."

"Thanks, Evie. I'm glad you're here too."

"Cheers to that!" She clinked her glass against mine. "Now zip it and soak up the moment."

Our phones chimed in unison. It was a text from Wanda. "Need u at cafe."

Suppressing a sigh, Evie typed out her response. "Can it wait? Long day."

The ellipsis bubble popped up, signaling an incoming reply. Finally, Wanda texted back: "Need u at cafe ASAP."

I groaned. My day had been one problem after another, and it seemed like Wanda was about to serve up another one. Knowing she would keep trying until I responded, I quickly thumbed a reply on my phone.

"OK. What's up?"

Wanda responded immediately. "Someone u need to talk to. Info re: Tawny."

Evie and I started toward the parking lot. "I hope this isn't another one of Wanda's crazy fantasies," I said.

"Well, it's a possibility. Remember that time she found a secret tunnel in the cafe's basement? It turned out to be an old broom closet."

"Let's cross our fingers this is more productive than the broom closet fiasco," I said, only half-jokingly. We could use a break, and I wanted to believe that whatever was waiting for us at the cafe would bring us closer to some answers.

But with Wanda, I never knew what to expect.

# CHAPTER 13

*T*he smell of curry greeted us the moment we entered the cafe. Wanda worked behind the counter, efficiently arranging cups and utensils as she prepared for the evening rush. She caught sight of us right away and enthusiastically waved us over.

Evie and I perched on stools at the counter. Wanda leaned in like she was about to divulge a state secret. "They call him Plummet," Wanda murmured, partially covering her mouth. Seeing our puzzled faces, she elaborated, "It's a nickname. The guy's real name is Shane Hayes. He's a local entrepreneur, a Chamber of Commerce acquaintance. We chatted about Tawny, and he's far from heartbroken about her death. Just give him a listen."

Evie and I traded a look. Maybe Wanda was onto something this time.

"That's him, right over there," Wanda said, discreetly pointing toward a guy in his late twenties, seated at a table by the window. He sported a scruffy beard and had sunglasses perched atop his messy brown hair. He appeared to be engrossed in his phone, and a tall glass of iced tea sat untouched in front of him on the table.

As we approached, Plummet glanced up from his phone to size us up.

"So, Wanda says you're interested in Tawny," he said, his tone indifferent. "Not sure why, but whatever. Pull up a chair."

With the smell of curry growing stronger by the minute, Plummet shared his story. He explained that he owned Rocks + Roots, a mountain bike shop that used to be located a few doors down from the mercantile. I knew the place, except it seemed like the business had changed names not long ago.

Plummet's agitation grew as he vented about Tawny. He insisted that she had deliberately targeted him and spun a tale about how her dog defecated in the same spot on his mother's sidewalk every morning. He even claimed to have evidence that she'd trained the dog to do it.

But what really irritated him was that Tawny had managed to convince his landlord to pull the plug on renewing his Main Street lease. Forced to scramble, he'd relocated Rocks + Roots to a half-empty strip mall on the edge of town—a definite downgrade. The new spot just didn't draw enough foot traffic for robust bike rentals, causing his sales to, ironically, plummet.

"Wait a minute," I interjected. "Isn't there still a bike shop operating at that location?"

"Well, that's the thing," Plummet said. "I wasn't gone a week before signs went up for a new bike shop. Alpine Adventure Bikes. Their rentals are pricey and the stuff they sell is high-end junk. Stupid name too. Sounds like someone made it up with one of those online business name generators."

"I'm not following," Evie said, her eyes narrowing. "No

offense, Plummet, but why would Tawny care about your bike shop?"

Plummet said Tawny had targeted him as part of her "Revitalize Beechtree" crusade. He admitted that his signs needed updating and his shop could be tidier, but he argued that was normal for a mountain bike shop. Tawny wasn't having it, though. She said his shop didn't live up to Beechtree's supposed "values," and warned him she'd shut him down if he didn't clean up his act.

The situation grew so dire that Plummet had hired an attorney. The lawyer told him Tawny didn't have the authority to close the shop based on clutter, but before Plummet could do anything about it, his landlord refused to renew his lease. And that was completely legal.

"Want to know the worst part?" Plummet asked. "Sales at my new location are so bad that I've had to start driving for Uber at night. Can you believe it? Uber! It's really put a damper on my nighttime routine at the Hop House, that's for sure."

"That's rough, Plummet. I'm sorry you're in this mess," I sympathized.

But Evie was incensed. "It's outrageous," she exclaimed. "People like us pour our hearts and souls into our businesses, and then someone like Tawny comes along and blows it all up."

"Tell me about it," Plummet agreed, "and I'm not the only business owner she stuck it to. Take Jenny at Jenny's Flower Shack. Tawny pulled the same stunt with her, and Jenny ended up spending a fortune on storefront renovations she couldn't afford."

"Did it get Tawny off her back?" I asked.

"Nope," Plummet answered. "Last I heard, Tawny was piling on new demands. I got the impression that whatever

Jenny did, it wouldn't be enough for Tawny. She pulled similar stunts with other local business owners."

Plummet shared more examples of how Tawny had pressured local business owners. She'd obviously wielded her influence in some questionable ways. Plummet's animated body language must have caught Wanda's attention because she sauntered over to the table.

"Wanda, did Tawny ever threaten you or the cafe?" I asked.

Wanda thought for a moment. "Well, she did push me to change the menu and give the place a facelift. She said it wasn't modern enough and threatened repercussions if I didn't comply. But I stood my ground, and she backed down eventually."

As I listened to Wanda, it dawned on me that Tawny might not have been as invincible as she'd appeared. Unlike her dealings with Plummet and other local business owners, she'd given Wanda a wide berth. Still, it was clear that Tawny had an agenda—the kind of agenda that made enemies.

I shifted in my chair. "Plummet, I'm not sure if you know this, but Tawny was found dead on my family's property, Loon Lodge. Heard of it?"

"Fuzz's joint?" Plummet's face lit up. "I love that place. Fuzz is such a cool guy. Did you know he gave me my first job? I worked at the lodge the summer after my junior year. Short-lived, though. Fuzz and I disagreed about whether it's appropriate to call in sick to shred trails."

"Yep, that's the place," Evie said. "Anyway, we're still trying to figure out what happened and . . . well, let's just say we're asking some questions."

"We're conducting an investigation!" Wanda blurted out, apparently unable to contain herself.

I shot Wanda a stern look. "It's not really an investigation.

Like Evie said, we're just asking questions. So, Plummet, any idea who might have wanted Tawny dead?" I asked.

He laughed. "Considering how she acted, I doubt anyone will miss her. I'm not gonna lie, I'm glad she's out of the picture. I just wish it had happened sooner. Trust me, I'm not the only one who feels that way."

Though I'd hoped Plummet would help us narrow down the list of suspects, I wasn't surprised when he said half of Beechtree had issues with Tawny. Before we went our separate ways, I thanked him for the information and insisted on paying for his meal as a token of our gratitude.

Wanda tempted us with some curry, but Evie and I both had to pass. Evie said she had another commitment, and I had a dinner date lined up with Sam. As we headed to the Birdmobile, I prodded Evie for details about her plans, but she stayed quiet.

"Evie's mystery man strikes again," I teased.

"Don't worry about me, Honey Palmer," she said, swatting my arm. "You've got enough on your plate right now without worrying about my love life."

I chuckled. "I guess you're right, but I'm not stopping until I meet this man of yours."

"We'll see about that," she said. "Don't hold your breath."

# CHAPTER 14

$\mathcal{E}$vie and I discussed Plummet's allegations on the drive back to the lodge. If even half of what he said was true, Tawny had been involved in some sketchy stuff.

"I still can't wrap my head around why Tawny wanted to shut down all those small businesses," I said. "It's not like she cared about revitalizing Beechtree. And why did she focus on businesses like the bike shop and flower shop?"

"I'm just as stumped as you are about Tawny's motives," Evie admitted. "But I think I know why she targeted businesses like the bike shop."

I raised an eyebrow. "You do? Enlighten me."

Evie shared her theory that Tawny had given the café and other established businesses a pass because they were popular with Beechtree voters. Instead, she had focused on low-hanging fruit, new arrivals like the flower shop or businesses that catered to out-of-towners with no say in local elections—like Plummet's bike shop.

"That makes sense," I said, steering the Birdmobile into the lodge's driveway. "It's a ruthless move, but it tracks with what we know about Tawny."

"I don't think Tawny chased Plummet away so she and George could open their own bike shop, though. Retail doesn't seem like their vibe," Evie added.

"I agree, but Tawny was all about making money. You can bet she found a way to turn a profit from the situation," I said.

We found Fuzz and Charley playing fetch on the side lawn. Charley's tail was a blur of motion, and his tongue lolled out of his mouth as he sprinted after his favorite toy: a red rubber ball with big hexagonal holes.

As Evie and I stepped into the yard, Charley snatched the ball in his jaws and bolted, daring Fuzz to chase him. Charley still had plenty of energy left, but Fuzz looked wiped out. His forehead shone with sweat, and his chambray work shirt drooped on his tired frame.

Fuzz signaled he was done, but Charley had no intention of giving up. He stopped a few yards away, the ball firmly clenched in his mouth, staring at Fuzz with puppy-dog eyes. Fuzz refused to take the bait. He collapsed on the porch steps and mopped the sweat from his brow with a red bandana he retrieved from his pocket.

"I'm beat," Fuzz declared, catching his breath. "What's up with you guys?"

We filled him in on our chat with Wanda and Plummet. He'd heard that Plummet had relocated his bike shop, but the news that Tawny had orchestrated his Main Street eviction was a revelation. He nodded along with our theory about Tawny targeting businesses that wouldn't ruffle the feathers of local voters.

"You're saying the lodge was next in her crosshairs because our guests can't vote?" he asked, stroking his beard as he pieced it all together.

I shifted my weight and crossed my arms. "Yeah, that's the theory," I confirmed.

Just then, Rupert from Cabin 2 sauntered over, looking like he'd just disembarked from a yacht at Martha's Vineyard. His pink polo shirt, seersucker shorts, and deck shoes weren't what I expected from a guy who claimed to sell heavy equipment to construction companies.

"What can I do for you, Rupert?" Evie asked.

"I hope I'm not being a nuisance, but it turns out I have to extend my stay one more night." He glanced nervously at his phone. "I've got a client issue to resolve before heading back."

Fuzz pushed himself to his feet. "All right, but you have to vacate early Friday morning, like we talked about. Your cabin's booked for the weekend."

"Thanks for the flexibility," Rupert responded. His cologne saturated the air. Its scent was almost overpowering.

I plugged my nose and seized the chance to learn more about his relationship with George. "So, Rupert, I was talking to George and he said the two of you go way back." George had actually said they'd just met, but I wanted to see if their accounts lined up. "How did the two of you meet?"

Rupert's lips curled into a smarmy grin. "Ah, well, I had no clue Tawny was the woman involved in that marsh accident. George and I were childhood pals, and it devastated me when I heard the news. We've drifted apart over the years, but I could tell you stories about the trouble George and I used to get into."

"I'll bet the two of you have been involved in some real hijinks," I said. It was a safe bet because I was pretty sure they were involved in some hijinks right now.

Rupert chuckled politely. "By the way, have you heard anything else about Tawny? I know the police are investigating her death, but I'm curious if you noticed anything out of the ordinary before the incident."

"Depends on what you call out of the ordinary," Fuzz said,

shuffling his feet. I could tell he was winding up to rant about Tawny.

"He's just kidding around," I said, cutting him off. "We actually didn't know Tawny or George very well."

"That's why we invited them to the lodge, to get to know them better," Evie added.

Before going back to his cabin, Rupert asked us to keep him posted if we noticed anything strange. He assured us he was just a good friend trying to help George find out what happened to Tawny.

"I think that might be the third time that guy has lied to us," I said as Rupert walked away. I recounted the story of how I'd caught Rupert lurking outside Tawny's cabin and reminded them that he'd lied about being an equipment salesman. I also shared what George had told me earlier, about how he had just met Rupert for the first time.

Fuzz resettled on the porch steps, propping himself up on his elbows. "Which one of them is telling the truth?"

"I don't trust either of them, but I'm more inclined to believe George," Evie said.

"I'm with you," Fuzz agreed. "Rupert's shifty." His eyes twinkled as he changed gears. "So, what do you have planned for this evening, ladies?"

Evie shot me an uneasy look. "We both have dinner plans."

"Evie's got a mystery boyfriend," I squealed, unable to keep the news to myself.

Fuzz sat up straighter on the steps. "Really? Is he a keeper?"

"Too soon to tell," Evie answered, "but we'll see how it goes."

Fuzz smirked. "Charley, what about you? Got any plans for tonight?"

At the mention of his name, Charley leapt up, drawing a

grin from Fuzz. "Guess it's another round of fetch for me." He wrestled the ball from Charley's mouth and launched it across the yard. Ecstatic, Charley barked and tore after it.

Evie and I locked up the lodge office then went to our cabin to freshen up. Along the way, we ran into Maddie and Liliana dressed for a night on the town.

Liliana dazzled in a blush pink blouse paired with dark-washed skinny jeans and black pumps. Her vibrant red hair was styled in loose curls, and she wore a delicate gold pendant necklace that added a touch of sophistication to her outfit. Maddie had opted for a breezy floral dress that fell just above her knees and beige wedge sandals. Understated makeup highlighted her blue eyes and full lips, and her sleek ponytail accentuated her cheekbones.

"You look amazing," I said. "What's the occasion?"

"It's date night, remember?" Maddie beamed. "We're off to Lake Placid for dinner and a late movie. What's new with you? Liliana mentioned the new theme for the festival, and it sounds pretty cool."

Evie filled them in on our latest findings, and Maddie assured us she'd spread the word among her ranger colleagues. She felt sure the new angle would pique their interest.

We then briefed them on our chat with Plummet. As it turned out, Liliana knew him from her mountain biking circuit, not to mention his almost daily excursions to the Hop House. While she described him as a nice guy, she also mentioned his penchant for conspiracy theories—like the time he tried to convince her that the moon served as a base for extraterrestrials.

"Maybe we can't bank on Plummet's story after all," Evie sighed.

"Hold on a minute," Maddie interjected. "Plummet may

85

have some weird beliefs, but that doesn't mean we should write him off entirely."

"Wait, didn't you say that you weren't getting involved in our investigation?" I asked.

"I'm not involved in anything," Maddie said. "I'm just a concerned citizen offering some friendly advice about a local situation."

"I doubt your boss would see it that way," I countered, giving her my best "mom's worried" expression. "You could lose your job over this."

"Thanks for looking out for me," Maddie replied. "But I can't just sit on the sidelines. I want answers as much as anyone else."

"Even so, I'd appreciate it if you didn't do anything that could get you in trouble," I said.

Maddie vowed to limit her involvement, and Liliana promised to stay alert at the Hop House for any chatter about Tawny or business owners she'd clashed with.

"Don't worry, Mom," Maddie said. "Everything will work out."

I returned her smile. "Let's hope so."

# CHAPTER 15

*I*'d arranged to meet Sam at seven, but he acted cagey when I asked him about our dinner plans. I could tell he had something up his sleeve, so I took a cue from Maddie and changed into a sundress and simple cardigan.

Before I left the cabin, I sent a quick text message to Childress, telling her that we remembered seeing Tawny's cell phone at dinner. I also texted the Fly Girls a summary of what Evie and I had learned from Plummet. With everyone on the same page, I climbed into the Birdmobile and started toward the campground, anxious to see what Sam had in store for us.

He was waiting for me outside the RV, looking relaxed and casual in a plain white t-shirt, jeans, and a pair of worn Birkenstocks. I suddenly felt overdressed in my sundress. I didn't want him to think I was trying too hard.

Then I saw what he'd done with the RV. Twinkling fairy lights draped the awning, and a flock of candles flickered on the cloth-covered picnic table. He had even arranged tiki torches in a circle around the outdoor seating space. In the center of the circle, a two-person camping couch, complete with cushions and fuzzy blankets, created a perfect spot to snuggle up and enjoy the night sky. To top it all off, flames crackled in the fire pit.

"This is incredible!" I exclaimed as my eyes took it all in. "You didn't have to do all of this."

Sam's face glowed. "I'm just happy you like it," he said, glancing over his handiwork. "I wanted our evening to be memorable."

He poured me a glass of wine and led me to the comfiest seat on the couch before disappearing into the RV. A few minutes later, he emerged with a tray of homemade sushi rolls. He'd obviously spent a lot of time and effort preparing the meal.

Sam fidgeted with his chopsticks as I ripped through my first sushi roll.

"Is everything all right?" I asked.

He took a deep breath. "To be honest, I can't stop thinking about our conversation at the Hop House last night. You said you're probably going back to Rochester at some point. Before you decide for sure, I want to try to convince you to stay."

I didn't know how to react. Sam and Beechtree were growing on me, but I still didn't see myself staying beyond the summer. I didn't want to hurt his feelings, so I didn't say anything. I just inched closer and reached out my hand, intertwining my fingers with his.

We sat quietly for a few minutes, staring into the fire.

"Okay, this is going to sound cheesy, but humor me," I said, remembering an exercise I'd learned in couples therapy with Kevin. "Let's close our eyes and picture where we see ourselves in five years. Then, if we feel comfortable, we can share what we saw with each other."

Sam had a skeptical look on his face, but he agreed to give it a shot. We each took a deep breath and closed our eyes.

In my mind, I envisioned the lodge bustling with activity again, like it did when I was a little girl. The laughter of guests echoed through the great room, mingling with the scent of burning logs in the fireplace. In my imaginary future, I saw myself surrounded by the people I cared about. Maddie, Evie, Fuzz, the Fly Girls—they were all there. And Sam was there too.

We opened our eyes. "What did you see?" Sam asked, his voice barely louder than a whisper.

"I saw a life where I'm happy and fulfilled, surrounded by the people I love," I said softly. "And maybe I'm starting to see how that might include you."

Sam's eyes lit up. "Me too," he beamed. "I just want to build a life with someone I care about."

As the night wore on, we talked about everything and nothing at the same time. We laughed, joked, and shared stories about our childhoods, our dreams, and our hopes for the future. We existed in our own little bubble, separate from the outside world. The fire slowly turned to embers, and we dozed off.

The vibration of my phone jolted me awake. Maddie's name flashed on the screen. Why was she calling me this late?

"Hey, what's going on? Is everything all right?"

"Not really." Maddie's voice was laced with alarm. "It's Fuzz. Big Ted and a deputy just showed up at his cabin. I think they're going to arrest him."

My heart pounded in my chest. "I'm on my way," I said, my voice tight. "Don't let Big Ted do anything until I get there."

I nudged Sam awake and told him what Maddie had said

as I gathered my belongings. He insisted on joining me, and we jumped into the Birdmobile and sped toward the lodge.

Arresting Fuzz was a low blow, even for Big Ted. Fuzz had argued with Tawny, and yes, he'd been on the property when she died. But none of that warranted slapping cuffs on him.

If Big Ted thought I was going to let him arrest Fuzz based on that weak sauce, he had another thing coming.

BIG TED'S police cruiser was parked outside Fuzz's cabin. Evie and Liliana stood nearby, restraining a visibly agitated Charley on a leash. Maddie paced back and forth, her arms folded tightly across her chest. I parked the Birdmobile and hurried toward them with Sam in tow.

"Big Ted and his deputy are inside with Fuzz," Maddie said. "He hasn't said much so far, only that he wants us to wait here."

Just then, Big Ted stepped out of the cabin. As he approached, Charley growled low in his throat, causing Big Ted to glance nervously in his direction.

Liliana offered to take Charley back to her cabin, but he dug his paws into the ground and refused to budge. After a little coaxing, he finally relented and allowed Liliana to lead him away, giving Big Ted one last warning growl as he padded off.

"I'm afraid I have some unpleasant news," Big Ted said, his face grim. "We're detaining Mr. Stillman on suspicion of murder."

Sam's face registered disbelief. "You can't be serious," he said. "Fuzz? A murderer? You're way off base here, Chief."

Big Ted glared at him. "Stay out this, Sam. You don't know what you're talking about."

"And you do?" I shot back. "Be honest, you made up your mind to pin this on Fuzz from the start."

Big Ted squinted at me. "My job is to follow the evidence, Ms. Palmer. And right now, the evidence is pointing directly at your father."

"But you're making a mistake!" Evie said, desperation in her voice. "We can prove that—"

Big Ted cut her off. "I don't have time for this." Without another word, he turned and disappeared back into the cabin.

A few minutes later, he and his deputy escorted Fuzz out of the cabin, hands cuffed behind his back. Fuzz looked defeated, his shoulders slumped and his eyes fixed on the ground in front of him. It broke my heart. I wanted to hug him and tell him that everything would be okay, like he'd done for me hundreds of times when I was a little girl. But this time, it involved something a lot more serious than a scraped knee or a C+ in chemistry.

Maddie pushed me aside to confront Big Ted, demanding to know what evidence he had linking Fuzz to Tawny's murder. Big Ted refused to talk details, but he insisted that he had legitimate reasons to suspect Fuzz's involvement. Then he and his deputy loaded Fuzz in the back of the police cruiser and drove away.

"What's our next move?" Sam asked.

Maddie didn't hesitate. "We need to find out what really happened to Tawny, and we need to do it fast. Big Ted arrested Fuzz on suspicion of murder, but he hasn't pressed charges yet. We need to clear Fuzz before he does."

I nodded in agreement. "Okay, where do we start?"

"The Fly Girls are our best chance at uncovering the truth," Evie said. "We can schedule a meeting at the lodge first thing in the morning."

"Good idea." I said, reaching for my phone. "I'll text the group right now."

Evie and Maddie retreated to their cabins, leaving Sam and me alone. With Fuzz behind bars, I needed to stay close to the lodge. So, I handed Sam the Birdmobile keys and told him to go back to the RV without me. He argued with me, of course, but I convinced him he couldn't do anything at the moment and promised to keep him posted about any new developments.

I found Evie waiting for me at our cabin. She smiled reassuringly. "Fuzz is gonna be fine. We just need to help Big Ted understand he didn't do anything wrong."

She seemed a lot more optimistic than I was about our ability to change Big Ted's mind about Fuzz. I couldn't shake the image of Fuzz being led away in handcuffs, but I pushed it aside to focus on the task at hand. We needed to find out what really happened to Tawny so we could clear Fuzz's name.

# CHAPTER 16

By seven the next morning, I had coffee brewing and a spread of bagels and muffins laid out in the lodge's great room, well ahead of the Fly Girls' eight o'clock meeting. I'd even thawed out the leftover blueberry cobbler and placed it on the serving table with the other pastries for the sugar fiends in the group.

Liliana and Charley showed up first. Charley immediately started sniffing around the great room, looking for Fuzz. When he couldn't find him, he whimpered and slumped onto the rug, looking as deflated as Liliana and I felt. I tried to console him with some ear rubs as the Fly Girls trickled in. Soon, we were all assembled in the great room, ready to talk about our next steps.

Well, almost everyone.

I'd tossed and turned most of the night, finally dozing off into a few hours of restless sleep. Waking up, I'd found a note from Evie saying she had to run an errand and that I should start the Fly Girls meeting without her. It seemed odd, but we both had a lot to do now that the festival was only two days away. I'd just assumed she'd woken up early to cross a last-minute detail off the list.

Maddie was a no-show too. Liliana said Maddie intended to join us, but she got called in for a search and rescue on Mount Ampersand. A day ago, I would have flipped out about Maddie coming anywhere near a meeting about Tawny's death. But with Fuzz behind bars, I realized I probably couldn't keep her away now if I tried.

I settled into an armchair and shared the story of Fuzz's arrest with the group. Liliana filled in additional details and offered the occasional expletive. Annie, on the other hand, sat quietly, knitting what looked like a cabled headband ear warmer.

When I finished talking, Annie set down her knitting and apologized for not warning us about Big Ted. She hadn't even known about Fuzz's arrest until Wanda called her. The reception desk at the police station was usually a hive of activity, so she didn't understand why she hadn't heard about it sooner.

Annie had really stuck her neck out keeping tabs on Big Ted for us. "Don't be too hard on yourself," I told her. "Big Ted knows we're friends. That's probably why he kept his plans to arrest Fuzz a secret from you."

"I'll bet we're all on Big Ted's radar now," Liliana speculated.

"That sounds about right," I agreed. "From now on, we've got to keep a low profile and stay out of sight."

"Out of sight, got it," Wanda echoed. "But the investigation is still going full throttle, right?"

"Well, before we hit the gas, we need a plan," I said.

Not surprisingly, each of the Fly Girls had their own opinion about what that plan should involve. After listening to their recommendations, some of which sounded illegal, I suggested we repeat the exercise I'd done the day before and jot down everything we knew. I grabbed a whiteboard from the lodge office, drew three vertical lines, and scribbled "Evidence" in the first column.

We started by going over the evidence at Warblers' End. Apart from the conclusions drawn by the medical examiner's report and Tawny's wet nightgown, there wasn't much. So far, I'd avoided mentioning the map we'd found in Tawny's cabin because I didn't want to step on Childress' toes. But with Fuzz in jail, it was time to lay all our cards on the table, so I filled them in.

Betsy slurped loudly on her hot chocolate. "That's it then. The only real evidence we've got is a wet nightie and a tourist map."

I reminded her about Tawny's missing cell phone but acknowledged that our physical evidence was thin. Returning to the whiteboard, I uncapped the marker and scribbled "Motive" in the second column. Since I'd already texted the group about our conversation with Plummet, I wasn't surprised to hear his name surface first.

"Plummet had a motive, all right," Wanda said. "Tawny cost him his sweet lease on Main Street."

Liliana nearly choked on her cobbler. "Come on. I know Plummet. He's weird, but he's harmless."

Annie raised her hand to speak. When I explained there was no need for hand-raising, she said, "It's not about whether we think Plummet is guilty or innocent, right? Even if he isn't the killer, he still has a motive for wanting Tawny gone."

"Annie's right," I said. "No one's saying Plummet did it, only that he had a reason to do it."

"In that case, add Fuzz to the list too," Betsy said, sending the group into an uproar.

Liliana sprang out of her seat and berated Betsy for daring to suggest Fuzz might have wanted Tawny dead.

Annie apologized for the umpteenth time before agreeing with Betsy, applying the same logic she used for Plummet. Wanda was on the fence.

I sympathized with Liliana's outrage. Leave it to Betsy to bring negative energy as a dish to pass. The only problem was that she had a point. Fuzz did have a motive.

"For now, we're just discussing motives, not pointing fingers," I said. "I agree with Betsy. Fuzz's motive is basically the same as Plummet's. Tawny threatened the lodge, and apparently, other businesses too."

"Like my cafe," Wanda said, "and Jenny's flower shop."

I wrote the words "threats to business" in the motive column.

"What about George?" Annie said. "Believe it or not, the true crime podcasts are right more often than you'd think. It's usually the spouse."

I told the group about my conversations with George and Rupert but noted that we had no information about their motives. The group suggested money and an affair as possibilities, so I wrote them on the whiteboard with question marks beside them.

Finally, I labeled the third column on the whiteboard "Suspects." To avoid another argument, I wrote Fuzz's name at the top of the list, then added the other names we had discussed.

"Fuzz, Plummet, Jenny, George, and Rupert," Betsy said. "One of them has to be the killer."

I shook my head. "Not necessarily. These are just the people we suspect based on the evidence we have so far." I drew a blank line at the bottom of the list with a question mark after it to emphasize my point. "The killer could be someone we don't know about yet."

"Okay, strategy time: divide and conquer," Liliana announced as she divvied up people to investigate. She assigned herself Plummet because they ran in the same social circles, and Wanda volunteered to chat with Jenny at the flower shop. Although Annie didn't know George very well, she promised to dig around the courthouse to learn more about his and Tawny's real estate dealings. That left Rupert for Evie and me to investigate.

"What about Fuzz?" Betsy asked.

Liliana raised an eyebrow. "Seriously? Big Ted is on Fuzz like a fly on honey. But if you really think Fuzz is the culprit, feel free to investigate him yourself."

"No need to bite my head off. I was just asking," Betsy responded. "I guess we can leave Fuzz to Big Ted. I'll go back to Warblers' End to double-check for any clues we might have missed."

After jotting down our tasks on the whiteboard, I steered the conversation toward festival preparations. Wanda's concession stand and the women-in-birding panel were all set. Liliana had already picked out spots for women-only birdwatching hikes, and everyone else was making good progress on their assignments.

Charley had lounged on his rug throughout our entire conversation. Out of nowhere, he perked up, lifting his head and sitting tall.

Then, as if on cue, Fuzz and Evie burst in through the side door. And they weren't alone. Maddie followed right behind them, along with her dad, Kevin.

My ex-husband.

# CHAPTER 17

The moment Charley spotted Fuzz, he bolted across the room, nearly knocking him over in a whirlwind of tail wags and slobbery kisses. Fuzz's face lit up as he reciprocated with ear scratches and belly rubs for Charley.

Ignoring Kevin for the time being, I turned to Fuzz. "What are you doing here?"

"I still live here, don't I?" he casually poured himself some coffee and settled onto the couch, Charley at his feet.

Evie sidled up next to him on the couch. She shared that Kevin had driven in early from Rochester to meet Maddie and her at the police station. After presenting himself as Fuzz's attorney and spouting some legal jargon, he'd met with Fuzz and then secured his release.

"Technically, Fuzz was released into my custody," Kevin clarified. He was dressed in his navy Brooks Brothers suit with a yellow tie and a white shirt with French cuffs. It was an outfit he called his power suit, the one he wore when he wanted to intimidate an opposing attorney or, in this case, a small-town police chief. I'd always thought the power suit seemed a little over the top when we were married, but for Fuzz's sake, I was glad he'd worn it today.

"Let me get this straight," Liliana said. "Kevin showed up and Big Ted let you walk out the door, just like that?"

"Yep, just like that," Fuzz repeated, staring into his coffee mug.

Kevin provided more details. "Big Ted's case against Fuzz was pretty weak," he said. "It was mostly a few witness statements about an argument Fuzz had with the victim. I convinced Big Ted to let Fuzz stay at the lodge while the police investigate, but I think it's safe to say he's no longer a suspect.'"

Liliana jumped up from her seat and snatched the dry-erase marker from my hand. With a bold stroke, she crossed out Fuzz's name on the whiteboard, eliciting a round of cheers from the group.

I was relieved to see Fuzz's name crossed off the suspect list. Still, I couldn't shake the feeling that Kevin's explanation didn't quite add up. The evidence against Fuzz was flimsy, for sure. But Big Ted was stubborn, and he wouldn't have released Fuzz without a good reason. There had to be more to the story. Kevin must have said or done something to change his mind.

As the meeting ended, the Fly Girls congratulated Fuzz one at a time. Annie felt compelled to explain why we had written his name on the whiteboard but assured him that we never considered him a serious suspect. Meanwhile, Wanda promised to whip up a chocolate cream pie, Fuzz's favorite dessert, as a reward for "breaking out of the joint." Even Betsy managed to eke out a few kind words before walking out the door.

After she left, Fuzz turned to me and Evie. "How about that? I would have gotten arrested a long time ago if I'd known Wanda would bake me a pie!"

∽

MADDIE AND LILIANA stayed to help with cleanup. We quickly packed up the leftover pastries, then washed and put away the dishes. With the kitchen sparkling, Liliana went to find Plummet and Maddie left to get ready for work, sheepishly admitting there were no lost hikers on Mount Ampersand. When I returned to the great room, Fuzz and Evie were waiting for me. Kevin was nowhere to be seen.

"Where's Kevin?" I asked.

"He's probably trying to sneak in a nap in one of the guest rooms," Evie replied. "He's planning to stay for a few days in case Big Ted gets any funny ideas."

"Great," I muttered. I didn't like the idea of having my ex on the premises, but Kevin knew his legal stuff. If Big Ted set his sights on Fuzz again, a good attorney would come in handy. As much as it irked me, keeping Kevin close might not be a bad idea. For a day or two, anyway.

Fuzz shifted awkwardly on the couch. "Hey, kiddo, there's something else we need to talk about." He scratched his head —a dead giveaway that he was about to drop something big.

"Okay, what's up?" I asked tentatively. Part of me didn't want to know. I wasn't sure I could take any more surprises.

"Kevin didn't tell the whole story about how he got me out of jail," Fuzz said.

"No kidding. Big Ted wouldn't have let you go you unless he had a good reason," I replied.

Fuzz squirmed some more. He was obviously building up to something uncomfortable. "It turns out I've got an alibi for the night Tawny got killed."

"An alibi?" I asked, flabbergasted. "Someone can account for your whereabouts the entire night?"

"The entire night," Fuzz confirmed. He emphasized the word "entire." Eww!

My jaw hit the floor. I knew Fuzz had attracted the attention of Beechtree's widow brigade since Mom had passed, but the thought of him being romantically involved with someone? I didn't want to think about my father's love life. Ever. As strange as it felt, I couldn't resist asking the obvious follow-up question.

"So, who's your alibi?"

"Me," Evie answered, and looped her arm around Fuzz in a way that made it clear their relationship had moved way past the friend zone.

Evie shared that she and Fuzz had bonded while working at the lodge, and they'd realized they had a lot in common. Evie had been looking for a companion ever since she'd sold her marketing agency, and Fuzz admitted that he'd been lonely too. Their friendship blossomed into dinner dates when I'd started spending more time with Sam.

"Then one thing led to another, and well . . . you can probably guess what happened next," Fuzz said.

Fuzz was Evie's mystery man. All the signs were there, and I felt a little foolish for not seeing it sooner. At some point, I'd have to process the fact that my father and best friend were engaged in a torrid love affair, but I had some questions first.

"Why didn't you mention your alibi to Big Ted when he questioned you after Tawny's murder?" I asked.

Evie shrugged. "We were still trying to figure out how to tell you when the Tawny thing happened. We never imagined Big Ted seriously considered Fuzz a suspect."

"Not that it's any of Big Ted's business anyway," Fuzz grumbled.

I couldn't argue with him there. "Does Maddie know? When did she find out?"

Evie said she'd noticed Maddie snooping around for a few weeks, but she'd only come clean with her after Fuzz's arrest. Evie and Maddie had arranged to meet Kevin at the police station to make sure I heard about their relationship from them instead of Big Ted.

"Just so you know, calling Kevin was my idea," Fuzz added. "Evie and I'd just sat down for a late dinner when Big Ted showed up, and I asked her to give Kevin a call. I knew you might not be thrilled about it, but I figured it was time to lawyer up. Like it or not, your ex-husband is the best lawyer I know."

"He's the only lawyer you know," I pointed out. "But you're right, he is pretty good at it."

Everything they said made sense, even the part about Evie and Maddie plotting behind my back to meet Kevin at the police station. It hurt knowing that Fuzz and Evie had kept their relationship secret from me, but they were entitled to their privacy.

"I'm happy for you guys," I said. "I'll need some time to wrap my head around it, but can we agree to be more honest with each other moving forward? No more secrets?"

They nodded their agreement.

"Hey, kiddo, are you hungry?" Fuzz asked me, raising his eyebrows. "I've got leftover chicken back at my cabin."

I grinned at his attempt to lighten the mood. Classic Fuzz. "Thanks, but Evie and I have to take a raincheck. We have a date with Rupert."

# CHAPTER 18

*I*'d just finished describing my dodgy plan to spy on Rupert. After hearing the details, Fuzz bowed out.

"Time to hit the road, Charley," he said.

"That's probably not a bad idea. You've already been arrested once this week," Evie snickered.

Fuzz and Charley headed for the door. "My thoughts exactly," he said as he walked away, leaving Evie and me alone in the great room.

Evie leaned back in her chair. The worn leather creaked as her fingers drummed a silent rhythm on the armrest. "Are you sure about this?"

"It's a gamble, but we don't have a choice, do we?"

I'd told her about our assignment to gather more information on Rupert. He was hiding something, and we needed to know what it was.

The plan was simple. Rupert had a routine—he left the lodge early each morning and didn't return until afternoon. Since he'd opted out of housekeeping, we had no idea what was going on inside his cabin. If Rupert stuck to his pattern, he'd be leaving the lodge shortly. That's when Evie would trail him in her RAV4 while I snooped around his cabin for clues.

Legally speaking, entering a guest's room for cleaning and maintenance was totally legit. Rummaging through their personal belongings? That was a different story. Yet despite the legalities, the potential reward outweighed the risks. If searching Rupert's cabin would help solve the case before the festival, I'd gladly let Big Ted slap the cuffs on me.

Evie waved her hand. "You know it's not a problem for me. I worked in marketing, so I love gray areas."

"I'm not worried either," I assured her. "Besides, you'll have eyes on Rupert the entire time. If he heads back to the lodge, just send me a text and I'll scoot right out of his cabin. Simple, right?"

After a long silence, Evie leaned forward. "Where do you and I stand on the Fuzz thing?"

I took a deep breath. It was a good question. "You have to admit, it's a lot to take in. I mean, you and Fuzz? It's gonna take some getting used to."

Evie flashed a reassuring smile. "I get it. It's a big change for all of us."

"I trust you, Evie, but I'm worried about how it might play out. For example, what if things don't work out between you and Fuzz?"

"The last thing I want is for our friendship to be affected by this. Your dad's a great guy, but if things don't work out between him and me, I won't let it come between the two of you. Or the two of us." She reached for my hand. "You're my best friend. No guy could change that, not even your quirky old man."

I still had questions about things like sleeping arrangements, but it was starting to feel like Fuzz and Evie's romance was just another curveball. I reminded myself that Sam was part of the equation too. I'd spent a lot of time with him lately, and Evie hadn't said a peep about it. Maybe both of our lives were changing a little bit.

Evie glanced at her watch. "It's go-time. I better hit the road if I want to tail Rupert when he leaves."

"Just be careful, okay? Don't pull any crazy stunts," I said.

"Of course. What's the worst that could happen?"

FROM THE PORCH, I watched Rupert's car ease down the driveway. Evie followed at a reasonable distance in her RAV4. To be safe, I waited a few minutes before picking up a housekeeping caddy and heading for Rupert's empty cabin.

The inside of the cabin was chaotic. All sorts of clothing —t-shirts, socks, and even a pair of pajama bottoms—littered the living area. The kitchen wasn't any better. Half-empty take-out containers covered the countertop, and a pile of crusty dishes sat in the sink.

I would have never guessed that Rupert was such a slob. He seemed so organized, but he obviously had a hidden side, and it was downright disgusting. As I surveyed the cabin, I found myself appreciating Sam's neat-freakiness a little more.

The kitchen table was a mess too, its surface buried beneath a mound of takeout menus and paperwork from Rupert's check-in. I felt a little guilty sifting through his papers, but I pushed the feelings aside and steered myself to the master bedroom.

That space wasn't any better than the rest of the cabin. More pieces of clothing lay strewn on the floor, the bed was a jumble of twisted sheets, and an assortment of empty snack wrappers and beer cans cluttered the nightstand. I groaned, imagining the Herculean effort it would take to clean this mess tomorrow.

The desktop was bare except for a single green folder. I opened it and discovered a variety of documents inside, all related to Tawny. There were financial records, phone logs, and a disturbing number of pictures of her. The angles of the photos made it clear that they were surveillance shots.

The staggering amount of detail in the folder floored me. Why would Rupert have compiled so much information on Tawny? He didn't seem like a stalker, but this was more than a passing interest. He was hiding something big.

I quickly reassembled the folder, making sure it looked untouched. On a whim, I opened it back up and took some cell phone photos before returning it to its place on the desktop.

As I stepped out of the bedroom, my heart jumped into my throat as the front door creaked open. I quietly closed the bedroom door behind me and dropped to my knees. When Rupert walked in, he found me crouched on the floor in the hallway outside his bedroom door, scrub brush in hand.

"What are you doing in here?" he barked.

Thinking quickly, I pasted a smile on my face. "Just starting to get the cabin ready for the next guest," I explained, gesturing to the area of the floor in front of me with the scrub brush. "There was a stain on the floor here, but this whole place needs some serious cleaning."

His eyes quickly scanned the room, then landed on me and my cleaning gear. I held my breath, hoping he had bought my shaky excuse.

"I like my privacy. That's why I didn't request housekeeping." His voice still sounded icy, but it was softening. "I'll be gone early tomorrow like we agreed. You can clean then."

I apologized and left as fast as I could, knowing I'd barely escaped getting caught.

What was Rupert hiding? And more importantly, what was our next move?

# CHAPTER 19

$\mathcal{A}$fter my close call with Rupert, I went to the lodge office to check for new bookings. We were full for the weekend, but after that, reservations remained sparse. With a murderer running amok at Loon Lodge, who would be crazy enough to reserve a room?

On the bright side, it seemed like our off-the-books investigation was gaining momentum. The evidence I found in Rupert's cabin directly linked him to Tawny. It didn't prove that he killed her, but it didn't look good.

Evie burst into the office. Her sunglasses sat at a crooked angle on the top of her head, and she was juggling her purse, a coffee cup, and a takeout bag from the Beary Good Cafe.

"Okay, small wrinkle," she said, dumping her things on the desk. "I thought Rupert was bunkering down for a while, so I zipped down to Wanda's café. When I got back, his car was gone. He didn't catch you snooping around, did he?"

"He caught me, all right," I grinned, "but I think he fell for my cover story. Now tell me where he went."

Evie slumped into a chair to catch her breath. "Would you believe he made a beeline for George's place? It wasn't a first-time visit either because he didn't ring the doorbell. He just waltzed right in like he owned the place."

I shared what I'd found in Rupert's cabin. Evie wasn't too keen about the clean-up job ahead, but she was as amazed as I was about the folder and the creepy surveillance shots.

"There's more," I said. "I kept an eye on Rupert's cabin after I skedaddled out of there. He only stayed for a few minutes before he ran back to his car, and he was carrying the green folder."

I could see Evie piecing it together in her mind. "He forgot the folder and had to go back to his cabin to retrieve it. Which means George probably knows about the stuff in the folder too."

Evie looked a little queasy. "Wow. This is big. I think we'll need to call in the cavalry. What about Kevin?"

"No way." I was positive Kevin would know exactly what to do. But logical or not, I didn't want him solving my problems for me. "We should tell Childress, the state police detective."

"She's a better choice than Big Ted, that's for sure," Evie agreed.

I pulled Childress's card from my pocket and dialed her number, switching to speakerphone so Evie could listen in. Childress picked up on the second ring.

"Hey, Detective, it's Honey Palmer from Loon Lodge."

"Hey, Honey. What's going on?" she asked, sounding as cool as ever.

I told her about the folder I'd found in Rupert's cabin, passing it off as a random discovery during a routine cabin cleaning. On impulse, I admitted Evie had trailed Rupert to George's place. I think Childress realized what we'd done, but thankfully she didn't press for details.

"Here's where it gets interesting," I continued. "Rupert left the folder at his cabin, and he came back to retrieve it. So, we think George knows about the folder too."

Childress fell silent on the other end of the line. "Are you saying both George and Rupert are mixed up in this?" she finally asked.

"Maybe," I confirmed. Then I relayed Rupert's bogus cover story about a career in equipment sales and explained how George had lied to me about his relationship with Rupert. "Something's going on between those two."

Childress agreed it was suspicious and promised to investigate. In the meantime, she warned us to stay away from George and Rupert.

After I hung up, I turned to Evie. "Now I guess we'll just have to wait and see what happens."

Evie and I tossed around the idea of going back to George's place to watch Rupert, but in the end, we nixed it. We'd caused enough trouble already, and we'd promised Childress we would keep our distance.

No sooner had we decided to stay put than Kevin appeared in the doorway. "Knock, knock. Got a sec, Honey?"

Evie gathered her things. "I'll leave you two alone," she said. "I should check on Fuzz anyway."

We both knew Fuzz didn't need checking on. Evie was just trying to give us some privacy. As I watched her walk out the door, I racked my brain for an excuse of my own. Nothing came to mind, so I moved on to my backup plan—keep it casual.

"How was your nap?" I asked.

"Pretty great, actually," Kevin said, sinking into Evie's chair. He was wearing a powder blue Hawaiian shirt with orange blossoms. When we were still together, he used to make a big deal about wearing tropical-style clothes on summer trips to Beechtree. It had started off charming, but now it felt kind of stale. Like our marriage.

Our relationship wasn't always stale. In the early years, everything had seemed almost perfect. Kevin thrived at his father's law firm, and I enlightened high schoolers about the mysteries of biology and the natural world. We were happy and in love. Life felt like a big adventure.

Then Maddie came along. Kevin was making more money than ever, and he became less enthusiastic about my teaching career. He wanted me to stay home with Maddie and be a full-time mother. I agreed at first, mostly because I loved spending time with my daughter, though I'd still planned to return to the classroom eventually.

Kevin had other plans. Even though he was a great dad, he'd started treating our family as an accessory to his career. Suddenly, I found myself caught up in a whirlwind of fundraisers and dinner parties. I helped raise a ton of cash for worthy causes, but the endless cycle of social gatherings felt shallow. The bright spot had been meeting Evie at a YMCA gala.

Around that time, birdwatching became my oasis. It was the one thing that belonged to me and me alone. I even roped Evie into joining a birding club in Rochester. Together, we'd slogged through marshes and woodlands in search of spotted sandpipers and yellow-rumped warblers and other species whose names made us chuckle. But every bird we saw was a reminder of the life I'd sacrificed for my relationship with Kevin.

Eventually, I reached my breaking point and filed for divorce. Kevin never understood it. When I inked the divorce papers eight months ago, I'd overheard him tell his attorney that it was just a phase and we'd get back together soon. Brilliant as a lawyer, but in matters of the heart he was completely clueless.

"How's life treating you, Kevin?"

"Swamped with work at the firm. Like usual," he replied as he examined his fingernails.

"Keeping yourself fed? Eating right?" Romance was off the table, but I didn't want the guy to starve to death.

"I manage," he answered, offering a courteous grin. "I've learned how to make a mean grilled cheese sandwich. What about you?"

I could tell he was fishing for me to admit my life was as miserable as his, filled with gloomy evenings and grilled cheeses. It would have been easy to lie, but I had no intention of faking sadness just to boost his spirits.

"I'm doing fantastic. Spending time with Maddie and Liliana has been amazing. And Evie and I have been busy working on the lodge and organizing the birding festival."

"Maddie mentioned the festival. You and your birdwatching." He never understood my avian pursuits.

As we talked, I became even more convinced that the divorce had been the right decision. Kevin was still focused on his law career and social scene, and I was starting a new chapter in my life. I didn't know where it would lead me, but I couldn't wait to find out.

He cleared his throat. "Now that we've had some time apart, how would you feel about giving our relationship another shot?" he asked. His eyes glimmered like a teenager who had finally mustered up the courage to ask his crush to the prom.

Maddie had stayed in touch with Kevin and sometimes visited him in Rochester with Liliana. I'd asked her not to tell him about my relationship with Sam and promised to break the news myself if things heated up. Now it was time to rip off the bandage.

I meant to break it to him gently, but the words just tumbled out. "I met someone. His name is Sam, and we've been dating for a few months now."

Kevin's face fell like a curtain. "Really? Is it serious?"

"It's early days, but it feels right," I replied. "Honestly? I think it's time for both of us to move on."

I could see the disappointment in his eyes, but he seemed to accept the fact that I was seeing someone else. Almost.

"Well, think about it, anyway," he said. "Maybe we can talk more about it later."

"We can talk, but there's zero chance we're getting back together," I said, trying to keep his hopes in check. "I appreciate you helping Fuzz, though. It means a lot."

After he left, I hung back in the office to finish up some odds and ends. Then I threw my bag over my shoulder and headed out. I was finally taking back control of my life, and man, did it feel great.

CHAPTER 20

*M*y stomach growled. Lunchtime. Between the Fly Girls meeting and spying on Rupert I'd lost track of time.

I briefly toyed with the idea of zipping over to the village and grabbing Sam for a quick lunch at the cafe. The thought of devouring one of Wanda's chicken pesto sandwiches sounded like heaven, but Sam still had the Birdmobile parked at his camper, and my festival to-do list loomed large. As tempting as a lunch date was, a quick sandwich would have to suffice.

Evie must have had the same idea because I found her in our cabin, happily munching on a tuna salad sandwich at the kitchen table.

"There you are. I was about to send out a search party." She pointed toward the fridge. "Saved you some tuna in case you're hungry."

I tossed my bag onto the sofa and headed straight for the refrigerator. "You're a lifesaver," I said, grabbing the remaining tuna salad from the fridge. "I'm famished."

"I bumped into Kevin outside. He said he was off to the

village for a bite to eat, but he didn't seem very happy about it." Evie hesitated for a moment before plowing ahead with the question that was really on her mind. "How did your talk go?"

I pulled a loaf of wheat bread from the pantry and began assembling my sandwich. "Believe it or not, he actually suggested we give the marriage another go."

Evie's eyes grew so wide I thought they might pop out of her head. "You're kidding!"

"Nope, he really went there," I said, layering tomato and lettuce on top of tuna salad.

"What did you say?" she prodded, eager for more details.

"Let's just say I shut that door fast. I made it crystal clear we're not rekindling anything, then I hit him with the news about Sam," I said, slapping a piece of bread on top and slicing my sandwich in half.

Evie chuckled. "Wow, that must've thrown him for a loop."

"He didn't say much, but I could tell it caught him off guard," I said, remembering the disappointed look on Kevin's face when I told him I was seeing Sam. "But I got the impression he still thinks he can wear me down."

"Well, good for you." Evie smiled approvingly. "You deserve someone who treats you right."

We finished our sandwiches, then turned our attention to our plans for the afternoon. Evie updated me on the status of the guest rooms and cabins. I was glad to hear every unit was sparkling clean and ready for guests, except for Rupert's cabin, which we would turn over the minute he checked out. For now, Evie planned to spend the afternoon organizing check-in materials and making sure everything was in place for the vendors.

While Evie hunkered down in the office, I'd assemble canopies and organize the outdoor area for the festival. We planned to set up the signs the next day, but I wanted to have all the tents pitched by nightfall.

I reminded Evie that we also needed to stay in touch with the Fly Girls. They were still our best chance of digging up information that could potentially connect George and Rupert to Tawny's murder.

With our afternoon plans in place, Evie and I went our separate ways. She returned to the lodge office, and I went to the shed next to Fuzz's cabin at the south end of the property. The lodge owned a few canopies for special events, but we'd borrowed several more from friends and neighbors and temporarily stored them in the shed.

I was relieved to see Fuzz's truck parked in its normal spot. The truck would make carrying all those canopies to the other end of the property a piece of cake. I didn't bother asking for Fuzz's permission. He always left the keys in the ignition, and I didn't want to risk waking him up. He got grumpy when he missed his afternoon nap.

As I was heaving tent canopies into the truck bed, Betsy traipsed down the path from her house to the lodge wearing her usual getup: a long-sleeved work shirt, khakis, and a green boonie hat. Betsy had harbored a deep-seated fear of the sun for as long as I could remember. I was all for a good sunscreen, but she elevated sun protection to an art form. Even on the hottest summer days, she bundled up like the forecast called for a blizzard.

"What's all this?" Betsy asked, eyeballing the canopies.

"Just borrowing Fuzz's vehicle to haul these tents over to the vendor area," I said as I heaved another canopy into the truck bed.

"Hmm, well, I have those tent stakes you wanted to borrow, but they're sitting on my kitchen table," she said.

"No worries, I'll swing by and pick them up later today." I

added tent stakes to my mental to-do list. "Where are you off to?"

"Warblers' End, to make sure we didn't miss any clues," she answered.

I remembered that Betsy had volunteered to search Warblers' End again at the Fly Girls' meeting. "Good luck. No stone unturned, right?"

"No stone unturned," Betsy repeated and headed in the direction of the marsh.

I finished loading the last of the canopies and drove them to the spot Evie and I had picked out for the vendors. It was located between the lodge and the marsh, and it featured a stunning view of the lake. With stakes and string in hand, I marked out the spots for each vendor. It was like a giant game of Tetris, making sure everything fit and flowed just right. Once I had the spots marked out, I donned work gloves and started setting up canopies.

The sun blazed overhead, but I didn't mind the heat. I'd always found working outdoors a lot more enjoyable than sitting in a stuffy office, regardless of the temperature. Besides, I was too busy setting up canopies to complain. Their bold colors popped against the lush green landscape, creating a stunning visual effect. Little by little, the vendor area transformed into a vibrant village, ready to welcome festivalgoers.

I found myself getting more and more excited as my little village took shape. The festival wasn't really about vendors or speakers or signage. It was about bringing people together and celebrating the beauty of the Adirondacks.

The summer before we'd lost Mom, Fuzz had hatched a plan for an epic Fourth of July picnic at the lodge. He'd envisioned an event where lodge guests and town folk mingled, sharing stories over great food, live tunes, and a sky lit up with fireworks.

Working with the lodge's modest budget wasn't easy, but Fuzz was surprisingly resourceful. He managed to sweet-talk a local band into playing for free and eked out enough money from the lodge's savings account to pay for both the chicken and fireworks. Town residents had pitched in and brought dishes packed with home-cooked flavors to share.

The day before the picnic, Fuzz, Mom, and I had worked tirelessly to set everything up. Mom had a knack for making even small gatherings seem super cool, but that Fourth of July picnic was more than just a good time. We felt like we were doing something important for the community, and I was proud to be a part of it.

As I wrestled another canopy into position, an odd noise floated in on the breeze. It sounded more like a human yell than an animal noise, and it was coming from the marsh.

My first instinct was to dismiss it as kids goofing off at Warblers' End. The marsh's remote location made it a haven for all kinds of teenage shenanigans. But something about the sound unsettled me, and I couldn't ignore it.

What I found at Warblers' End sent a shiver down my spine. Betsy lay unconscious on the ground next to the bird blind. Her unmistakable boonie hat sat nearby, and she was bleeding profusely from a head wound. My heart beat out of my chest as I processed the disturbingly familiar scene.

Was this really happening again?

# CHAPTER 21

*O*nce more, lights and sirens lit up Loon Lodge. Minutes after I dialed 911, a fleet of emergency vehicles rolled into Warblers' End from the lodge side of the marsh. Big Ted led the pack, with a state police car right behind him.

While the EMTs worked on Betsy, I told Big Ted and a state police officer everything I knew. Well, almost everything.

Betsy was conscious when I found her, but her speech was jumbled and difficult to understand. I managed to piece together that she had spotted something in the weeds near the bird blind and decided to take a closer look. Next thing she knew, someone whacked her on the head with a heavy object, like a rock or maybe a tree branch. She could probably provide more details once she regained her senses.

Naturally, Big Ted wasn't satisfied.

"Where were you at the time of the incident?"

"Setting up canopies for the festival."

"Can anyone vouch for your whereabouts?"

"Probably not."

"Any idea who might have done something like this?"

Tricky question. George and Rupert seemed likely candidates, but I was reluctant to share my suspicions with Big Ted. No telling what chaos he'd unleash with that info. I trusted Childress and the state police a lot more than Beechtree PD.

"You should probably reach out to Detective Childress," I said, turning to the statie. "She's already investigating the death that happened here a few days ago, and she might have some additional information for you."

Big Ted bristled at my suggestion. He launched into a rant about jurisdiction, but the state cop cut him off and told me I was free to go. I watched as he dialed a number on his phone, taking a few steps away from Big Ted to make the call.

Perfect. Childress had promised to take a closer look at George and Rupert. With any luck, she'd tie them to Betsy's attack and have them both in custody before the festival.

As I made my way back to the lodge, I ran into Evie, Maddie, and Liliana on the path to Warblers' End. Annie had heard about Betsy on the police radio and texted the others on the Fly Girl's thread.

"How's Betsy?" Evie asked.

"Not great. She took a pretty serious blow to the head," I said, then I repeated the story I'd told Big Ted and the state cop a few minutes ago.

Liliana placed her hands on her hips. "We're all thinking the same thing, right? Rupert and George are the likely suspects here."

"Yeah. I think it's possible Rupert and George are tied to both Tawny's murder and Betsy's attack," I agreed. "But how did you know those two were on our radar?"

Evie casually waved her hand. "I told Maddie and Liliana about the stuff we found in Rupert's cabin," she explained. "What was Betsy doing at Warblers' End anyway?"

"She volunteered to search Warblers' End for more clues," I said, remembering that Evie and Maddie had missed that part of the Fly Girls' meeting. "It didn't seem like a very risky assignment at the time."

Maddie had a puzzled look on her face. "I'm not making the connection. Why would Rupert and George want to hurt Betsy?"

Liliana hypothesized that Rupert and George might have followed Betsy to Warblers' End, then bopped her on the head when she stumbled across an incriminating piece of evidence. She couldn't explain why Rupert and George were following Betsy in the first place, but it was as good a theory as any.

"Maddie, you were with me at Warblers' End the morning after Tawny's murder. Big Ted and his deputy searched the entire scene, right?" I asked.

"Yeah, they combed every inch of Warblers' End," Maddie confirmed. "Other than Tawny's body, the only thing that turned up was the empty bottle I found. And the police have that now."

"Do remember what kind of bottle it was?" Evie probed.

"Yeah, it was a sparkling wine bottle. I think the label read 'Dancing' something," Maddie answered.

"Dancing Daisy?" Liliana interjected.

Maddie nodded. "That's the one. I hadn't heard of it before."

Liliana wrinkled her nose. "It's bottom-shelf swill. Definitely not Tawny's style. My guess is that it was probably left over from a teenage drinking party."

Just then, emergency vehicles and police cars approached us from the direction of Warblers' End. We stepped aside so they could pass, feeling powerless as an ambulance carted off one of our own.

"Well, at least Betsy is going to be all right," Evie said, breaking the tension.

"That's what the EMTs said. She'll probably have to spend the night at the hospital for observation, but she'll bounce back." The fact that Betsy would recover didn't make me feel any better about the situation.

Maddie read my mind. "Are you okay, Mom?"

"I'm fine." The truth was that I felt responsible for Betsy's attack. I'd dragged the Fly Girls into this mess because I was determined to save the festival. If it wasn't for me, Betsy would be home right now, hanging out with Mr. Whiskers.

As we walked the rest of the way back to the lodge, I thought about our next steps. Childress was the key. Once she connected the dots between George and Rupert, the people responsible for Tawny's murder would be behind bars, and we could finally put this whole ordeal behind us.

My optimism evaporated when I saw the mayhem unfolding on the lodge's lawn. Kevin and Sam stood toe-to-toe, red-faced and shouting at each other, while Fuzz tried his hardest to prevent a full-on brawl.

When I was younger, the thought of two men fighting over me might have seemed flattering. But now, seeing my boyfriend and my ex-husband ready to throw punches, I felt more annoyed than anything else.

I darted between Kevin and Sam. "That's enough!" I snapped, channeling my angry-parent voice. "I don't know what's going on here, but everyone needs to calm down right now."

Kevin glared at Sam. "What do you see in this guy, Honey?"

"Hey, take it easy, man," Sam shot back. "You had your chance, and you blew it."

"Not helping," I sniped at Sam, my voice sharper than I

intended. "In case you didn't notice, Betsy just got hauled off in an ambulance."

"Fine," Kevin grumbled, backing off. "But this isn't over." With that, he stormed up the stairs and disappeared into the lodge.

Sam's expression softened. "I'm sorry, I didn't mean for things to get so heated. For what it's worth, he started it."

Frustration seeped into my voice. "Kevin has always had a short fuse. I was hoping you would be the bigger person here, Sam."

And just like that, it was over. Sam strode off to his Jeep and drove away without saying goodbye. Fuzz and I traded looks, acknowledging the awkwardness of the situation, while Evie, Maddie, and Liliana stood dumbstruck on the lawn.

"I bet no one had that on their Bingo card today," Fuzz said.

I ran my fingers through my hair. "I can't deal with this drama right now."

We needed to get our act together. The only problem was that I had no idea where to start.

# CHAPTER 22

*M*addie and Liliana couldn't leave fast enough. They said they had to go back to work and practically sprinted to the parking lot. Then Fuzz and Evie offered some obligatory words of encouragement and disappeared into the lodge.

Standing alone on the lawn, I realized that I'd dropped everything when Betsy was attacked and needed to finish setting up the tent canopies. Maybe a little physical labor would take my mind off things, and it did, for a while anyway.

But once the last canopy was standing among the others in the festival space, I found myself searching for another distraction. There were still plenty of items on our festival to-do list, but my heart just wasn't in it. Instead, I shuffled back to my cabin, filled a large thermos with iced tea, and headed to the gazebo.

There was nothing quite like Beechtree Lake on a summer afternoon. If the weather was calm, the surface glimmered like twinkling lights in a mirror. On any other day, I would have marveled at the beauty of it. But everything felt off-kilter now. Especially my relationship with Sam.

I flopped onto a weathered bench in the gazebo and took a big swig of iced tea from the thermos. News travels fast in a small town like Beechtree. I could see how Sam might have heard there was an incident and rushed to the lodge. Once he showed up, Kevin would've quickly pieced together that Sam was my boyfriend and tossed out a snarky comment to bait him into a spat.

Maybe I'd been too hard on Sam. I hadn't meant to hurt his feelings. I'd just wanted to prevent a physical altercation.

Taking another sip of iced tea, I let the sounds of the lake wash over me. The gentle lapping of the water against the shore, the cry of a seagull, and the distant murmur of traffic on the highway mesmerized me, and I drifted off.

I dreamed I was a little girl, fishing on the lake with Fuzz and my mother. The sun was shining, the birds were singing, and the water was crystal clear. Fuzz sat in the back of the boat, casting his line into the water. My mother sat in the front, reading a book. I was in the middle, holding my fishing pole—a Scooby Doo rod—hoping that a fish would like the look of the nightcrawler at the end of my line.

I could feel the sun on my face and the wind in my hair. I could smell the fresh air and the water. I could hear the waves lapping against the boat. I was so happy to be there with my family, enjoying the day.

We'd been out there for a while without so much as a nibble. I was ready to give up when I felt a tug on my line. Reeling it in, I discovered a small panfish on the hook. It was my first fish, and I was over the moon.

Smiling from ear to ear, I showed the panfish to Fuzz and my mother. They said they were proud of me, and we took a picture of me holding the fish before we released it back into the water.

I woke up with a smile on my face. It was just a dream, but it felt incredibly real. And I felt that easy, breezy happiness I used to feel when I was young.

"Mind if I join you?" Childress appeared beside me out of nowhere.

"Of course not," I said, gesturing toward an empty bench. "I'd offer you some iced tea, but I didn't bring any extra cups."

"No problem," she said. Grabbing the thermos out of my hand, she unscrewed the lid and drew a sip. "It really is beautiful here. I can see why you're working so hard to save this place."

"That's the idea," I said with a sigh. "But we don't seem to be making a lot of progress. Did you hear what happened at Warblers' End today?"

Childress nodded. "I was at another crime scene when I heard the call. I know you gave our officer your statement, but what happened?"

I recounted the same story I'd shared with everyone else. I told her that Betsy had mentioned seeing something in the weeds just before she was attacked, but when I'd checked the area, there was nothing there.

"Maybe Betsy's imagination got the best of her," I said. "Or maybe whoever hit her on the head took the evidence with them."

"That would be just our luck." She sounded genuinely disappointed. "I really wish we had more to work with than the information from the medical examiner's report."

"And the bottle," I added.

She looked confused. "What bottle?"

I explained that Maddie had uncovered an empty wine bottle at Warblers' End where we'd found Tawny's body, and that Big Ted had taken it as evidence. The fact that Childress didn't know about it made me momentarily question her abilities as a cop, especially since it was sitting in a police evidence locker.

"Big Ted didn't mention any bottle," she said, her voice laced with irritation. "He wasn't happy when we took over his investigation, but I'll give him the benefit of the doubt and assume he just forgot to tell us about it. I'll make sure to remind him before I leave Beechtree today."

For some reason, I didn't think it would be a very friendly reminder.

"The bottle might not matter anyway," I said. "What about George and Rupert? Are you ready to make an arrest?"

"Well, that's why I'm here," Childress answered.

My nerve endings tingled. The police were finally ready to bring Tawny's murderer—or possibly, murderers—to justice.

"Great! I'll bet Rupert's still holed up over at George's place. If you move fast, you can probably arrest them both at the same time," I said, my voice giddy.

"You misunderstood me, Honey. I'm not here to arrest anyone. In fact, we've cleared George and Rupert as suspects," Childress replied.

Her words knocked the wind out of me. "There has to be some kind of mistake," I insisted. "I'm positive George and Rupert are tangled up in this, especially Rupert."

"I understand your frustration," Childress said. "Technically, I'm not supposed to discuss the case with you." She glanced both ways to make sure we were alone. "But considering the circumstances, I'll tell you what I know."

After I'd told Childress about Rupert's file, she'd run a background check and quickly discovered that our suspicions about Rupert were spot on. He wasn't a heavy equipment salesman, but rather a private investigator based out of Albany.

Armed with that information, she'd driven to Beechtree

and interviewed Rupert and George separately. She'd learned that George and Tawny's marriage was in trouble. Over the past few months, Tawny had started to withdraw from George, sometimes disappearing for days at a time without explanation.

When George saw a divorce looming on the horizon, he hired Rupert to investigate Tawny. He wanted to know if she was having an affair, but he'd also asked Rupert to take a closer look at her business dealings. Rupert checked into Loon Lodge to keep an eye on Tawny and maybe even snoop around her cabin if he got the chance—ironically, the exact same thing I'd done to him.

"George and Tawny were joined at the hip in their real estate business," I said. "Wouldn't he have known about her financial dealings?"

"Not necessarily," Childress responded. "While George can access their joint accounts, he believes Tawny was exploring separate real estate deals and stashing money in a different account."

"So, the whole time Rupert was just trying to dig up information that George could use against Tawny in divorce proceedings?"

"That about sums it up," Childress said, helping herself to another gulp of tea from the thermos. "When Tawny turned up dead, George added her murder to the list of things he wanted Rupert to investigate. You saw them arguing, right? Rupert refused to investigate her murder unless George doubled his fee, which George eventually agreed to do."

Unfortunately, the pieces fit together. Rupert's lies, George's lies, the files in Rupert's cabin, George's strange behavior at Warblers' End. All the things that pointed to Rupert and George's involvement in Tawny's murder were simply the actions of a jilted husband and the private investigator he hired to dig up dirt on his soon-to-be ex-wife.

"You're absolutely sure they weren't involved?" I asked, frowning.

She sighed, "I've got a few more things to verify, but so far, their stories hold water. Sorry, I wish I had better news."

"Did Rupert find anything worth mentioning, at least?" I asked.

Childress hesitated. "I'm really not supposed to get into the specifics," she said. "This is still an active murder investigation, after all. But I can tell you that Rupert didn't find any evidence Tawny was having an affair. Whatever she was hiding had to do with business, not romance."

She went on to explain that George and Tawny's real estate business had made a negligible profit helping a few landlords find new retail tenants. However, George wasn't aware of any grand money-making scheme on Tawny's part. And while he admitted that her community revitalization effort was ethically ambiguous, it wasn't illegal.

"George is convinced that whatever Tawny was involved in was bigger than just closing down the local bike mountain bike rental shop," she said.

I looked out over the lake, lost in thought. Now that I had the facts, I had to agree with Childress. George and Rupert probably didn't murder Tawny.

But if they didn't kill her, who did?

# CHAPTER 23

*A*ll I wanted to do was relax and unwind. A hot shower, a glass of wine, and a good mystery novel sounded like the perfect way to do it. After the day I'd had, who could blame me?

So far, I'd wrangled my ex-husband, discovered that my father and my best friend were engaged in a torrid love affair, illegally spied on a lodge guest, dealt with the aftermath of poor Betsy's attack, and learned the police had no suspects in Tawny's murder.

But my day wasn't over yet. With Rupert's cover blown, he had probably reconsidered his plan to stay at the lodge an extra night. I had a hunch he was already on his way back to Albany, which meant I could get a head start on cleaning his cabin.

Sure enough, the door to Rupert's cabin stood wide open. His belongings were gone, but the cabin still looked like a disaster zone. I cursed under my breath and dragged the housekeeping cart out of the shed.

Combing through the mess, I found pizza boxes from the Hop House, burger wrappers from a local fast-food joint, and empty Chinese takeout containers. The kung pao beef container mystified me. The nearest Chinese restaurant was four towns away.

Evie and Fuzz strolled in while I was washing Rupert's dishes. Fuzz grimaced as he looked around the cabin. "What a mess."

"I tried to warn you," Evie said. "Rupert might look like he belongs on the cover of GQ, but he's really just a big old slob."

Fuzz snorted in disgust. "Ain't that the truth. It looks like he had a frat party in here."

Charley went straight for the kitchen garbage can. He took a few quick sniffs, then trotted back toward fresh air, settling down on the rug just inside the doorway.

I pointed to the pile of takeout containers littering the counter and table. "Any chance you want to help me take out the trash?"

The three of us made short work of the kitchen. From there, I moved on to the bedroom, while Fuzz tackled the bathroom and Evie vacuumed the entire cabin, room by room.

With Rupert's cabin ready for the next guest, the three of us regrouped on the lodge porch. Evie produced a bottle of Chardonnay, a Hop House IPA for Fuzz, and a bowl of fresh water for Charley. As we enjoyed our drinks, I could tell Evie was anxious to hear about my conversation with Childress.

I cleared my throat. "Detective Childress stopped by."

"About time you brought that up," Fuzz exclaimed. "I saw you sneak off to the gazebo, so I steered her your way. Then a few minutes later, Rupert showed up and cleared out his cabin in a big hurry. I knew something was up, so spill it."

Evie jabbed an elbow into Fuzz's ribcage. "We don't want to be nosy, but we're dying to hear what she said."

"Well, the punch line is that the police have officially cleared both Rupert and George as suspects," I said.

Fuzz's jaw hung open. "Are you serious? Rupert's as slippery as a lake trout, and George isn't much better."

"Maybe. But when it comes to Tawny's murder, they're off the hook." I summarized my conversation with Childress and shared the news that Rupert was a private investigator George hired to spy on Tawny.

"I knew it!" Fuzz jumped up, spilling beer on his shirt. "I told you Rupert didn't know squat about equipment. That explains why he acted so shifty around us."

"Why would George want to spy on Tawny?" Evie asked, sipping her wine.

I told her that George and Tawny were getting a divorce and even though Rupert hadn't found evidence of an affair, Tawny's unexplained absences and erratic behavior suggested she was up to something.

"Like what?" Fuzz asked, taking a quick swipe at the beer stain on his shirt.

"Hard to tell, but George thinks Tawny was hiding some kind of secret real estate venture from him."

Evie set her wine glass down and leaned back. "If I had some big business deal in the works, I'd probably want to keep it hidden from my soon-to-be ex-husband too," she said.

Fuzz took another swallow of beer, finishing off the bottle. As he wiped his mouth with the back of his hand, a little belch slipped out. "Where does that leave us?"

My shoulders slumped and I let out a sharp breath. "Back at square one."

Evie corrected me. "Not exactly. What about the local businesses Tawny closed?"

"The police know all about Plummet and the other small business owners Tawny pushed out," I said. "Strange as it sounds, the prevailing theory is that her efforts to revitalize Beechtree were semi-legit."

Fuzz laughed out loud. "Tawny was a lot of things, but a do-gooder wasn't one of them. Trust me, there's more to that story."

He was probably right. Although Tawny's real estate agency didn't significantly benefit from her actions, even George thought she had an agenda. Still, I reminded them that Annie, Liliana, and Wanda were investigating the business owners Tawny forced out of business. It was possible one of them had decided to get revenge.

"I hate to say it, Honey, but time's running out. People are asking questions, and we need to sort this out soon," Evie said. Our phones buzzed in unison. "Speak of the devil."

I pulled my phone from my pocket and a message from Annie popped up on the screen. "Need to talk. Can u guys swing by the Hop House in 20?"

My perfectly relaxing evening would have to wait a little longer.

# CHAPTER 24

*S*ince Sam still had the Birdmobile parked at his camper, Evie chauffeured us to the Hop House in her RAV4. The parking lot overflowed with vehicles, as if the entire town had suddenly developed an appetite for craft beer and pub grub.

Inside, a group of middle-aged musicians called Neon Rebellion performed Bon Jovi's "You Give Love a Bad Name." Judging by the packed parking lot, their loyal fan base had turned out in full force. I wasn't surprised. Neon Rebellion's fans rarely passed up an opportunity to groove to the band's '80s beats.

I spotted Annie at a table in the back. Her hands busily worked knitting needles and a half-empty beer glass sat nearby. She gestured for us to join her. As I sat down, it dawned on me that we were sitting at the same table where Sam and I'd had our most recent date night.

I still felt bad about the way we had ended things at the lodge, so I hatched a plan to have Evie drop me off at Sam's camper after we left the Hop House. When the server took our drink orders, I asked for an everything pizza to go as a peace offering. It was Sam's favorite, and I hoped it would help smooth things over between us.

"Thanks for meeting me," Annie shouted over the music. "Has anyone heard how Betsy's doing?"

"I called the hospital before we left the lodge," Evie said. "The on-duty nurse said she's sedated and sleeping like a baby. They expect to release her tomorrow."

"That's a relief," Annie said. "So, Honey, I heard you had a visitor this afternoon."

"You mean Detective Childress, right?"

The server returned with our drinks. Evie and I had already polished off glasses of wine at the lodge, so we'd switched to the house root beer for this round. Annie, however, went for something with more punch.

She lifted her glass of hop house lager and took a hearty sip. "Childress stopped by the station after she left the lodge."

I told Annie what Childress had learned about George and Rupert and confirmed that she'd planned to swing by the police station to collect the empty Dancing Daisy bottle Big Ted was holding in evidence.

"Did Big Ted hand the bottle over?" I asked.

"Oh, absolutely," Annie said, her eyebrows arching. "But not before she gave him a serious earful for not turning it over sooner."

Neon Rebellion finished their medley of Bon Jovi tunes and launched into Queen's "Another One Bites the Dust." Annie shifted in her chair.

"There's been a development," she continued, "and it's a classic good news, bad news kind of thing. I hate delivering bad news, so let's get that part out of the way. Big Ted wants to shut down the festival."

"He wants to do what?" Evie exclaimed, loud enough to attract the attention of diners sitting at nearby tables.

Annie explained that the Betsy thing had thrown Big Ted

for a loop. "He has no suspects and he's convinced there's a serial killer on the loose in Beechtree. When Childress showed up at the station, Big Ted accused her of dragging her feet and said it was her fault Betsy was attacked. Then he announced that he was shutting down the festival until Tawny's murderer is in custody."

I understood why Betsy's attack might raise concerns about the festival. But the facts didn't support Big Ted's random psychopath theory. It seemed like Tawny had gone to Warblers' End voluntarily, and that meant she'd probably known her killer. There was no real threat to festivalgoers and no reason to cancel the festival.

Annie and Evie agreed with me. In fact, Annie said Childress made the same argument to Big Ted, but the more Childress reasoned with him, the more adamant he became about shutting us down.

"If that's the bad news, what's the good news?" I asked.

Annie's freckled face broke into a smile. "That's when Childress brought up the bottle. She really put the fear of God into him, and he agreed to hold off for now. But if there's another incident, it's all over."

Though I was glad to hear the festival was still on, I knew Big Ted still had plenty of time to change his mind.

The waitress returned with Sam's pizza and the bill. I grabbed the tab and thanked Annie for sharing the scoop about Big Ted. Drinks were on me tonight. As Evie and I made to leave, Annie stopped us.

"There's something else." The tone of Annie voice made my stomach sink. "It's about Sam."

Evie and I settled back into our seats. "What does Sam have to do with all this?" I asked, leaning my elbows on the table.

"Probably nothing," Annie said. "But after the Fly Girls' meeting this morning, Wanda and I started asking around about Tawny's business dealings. Wanda struck out, so I decided to call up my friend Kathy at the County Clerk's office. It was a long shot, but I thought, why not?" Anyway, Kathy has a friend in the Public Works department who happens to live across the street from Sam's house in town."

I'd only been to Sam's house in the village a few times. We usually met at the RV, but he'd always described his street as a peaceful place.

"Sam says it's a quiet neighborhood, the kind of street where everyone gets along," I said, swirling my paper straw in my root beer.

Annie paused for a moment, choosing her words carefully. "I'm sure it is," she finally said. "It's just that Kathy's friend noticed Tawny coming and going from Sam's place a few times. I hate to be the one to tell you this, but I figured you should know."

My hand froze mid-swirl. "Did Kathy's friend say when it happened?"

"A few months back," Annie answered, sipping nervously at her own drink. "She didn't think it was important then, but she remembered it after she heard about Tawny."

Evie's eyes met mine. "Don't read too much into it. Like Annie said, it's probably nothing. I'll bet there's a rational explanation."

I nodded, but I knew we were all thinking the same thing. If Sam and Tawny weren't in cahoots, then they were having an affair.

I didn't know which one was worse.

# CHAPTER 25

*B*ack in the RAV4, Evie hesitated before turning her key in the ignition. "Honey, I'm speechless. I know how much you care about Sam."

I shrugged. "We haven't been together very long. No big deal."

Evie saw through my lame attempt to downplay my relationship with Sam. "I meant what I said. There are probably a dozen reasons why Tawny might have stopped by Sam's house."

I really wanted to believe her. But we both knew Tawny didn't visit Sam's house for afternoon tea. I felt angry and betrayed. And I felt like an idiot for believing the stuff Sam said about us having a future together.

"What now?" Evie asked, starting up the RAV4. "Do you still want me to drive you over to Sam's RV?"

"I guess so," I said. "I don't want to see Sam right now, but the longer I wait to get my car back, the more awkward it'll be."

We found the Birdmobile parked next to Sam's Jeep. Evie

offered to wait for me while I retrieved the keys from Sam, but I sent her on her way. I had to do this alone.

Holding the pizza box, I rapped on the RV's door with my free hand.

The door swung open almost immediately. "Hey there, stranger," Sam said. "Is that pizza for me?"

"My keys, Sam," I said. My tone was all business.

He looked stunned. "Uh, sure." Fumbling in his pocket, he threw the keys to the Birdmobile onto the pizza box. "Something wrong?"

"You could say that," I shot back.

His face shifted from surprise to bewilderment. "I'm confused. What are we talking about?"

"You and Tawny. Hanging out at your house. And there I was, trusting you."

He stepped out of the RV. "Hold on. Is that why you're upset? You don't understand—"

"You're right. I don't understand," I said, shoving the pizza box into his hands. "Enjoy your dinner."

Perplexed, Sam took the pizza as I spun on my heel and stormed back to the Birdmobile. Once inside, I drove aimlessly around Beechtree. My journey to nowhere ended at a small park on the outskirts of town.

As I sat on a bench in the park, the fading daylight cast soft hues of blue and pink across the sky. A red-winged blackbird sang from a nearby bush, its song sweet and uncomplicated.

If only the rest of my life could be that simple.

RETURNING TO THE LODGE, I parked the Birdmobile next to Evie's RAV4 and headed straight for a hot shower and comfy bed. I was tired in every way possible, but when I noticed the lights were still on at Maddie and Liliana's cabin next door, I decided to pop in.

I rapped lightly on the cabin door, catching faint laughter from inside. Maddie appeared and behind her, I saw Kevin sitting at the kitchen table, shuffling a deck of cards.

"I didn't realize you had company," I said, taking a step back. "I just wanted to check in, but I can swing by tomorrow morning."

"No, stay!" Maddie insisted. "Seriously, join us for a quick card game or something."

I really wanted to spend some quality time with Maddie, but fending off a needy ex-husband wasn't on my agenda. Before I could decline, Maddie seized my arm, ushered me in, and poured a glass of wine faster than you could say "Uno." I'd barely picked up my glass when she dealt me into the next round.

Surprisingly, the wine—or maybe the nostalgia—did the trick. Playing Uno around the table felt like a cozy flashback. When Maddie was eleven, I'd stumbled upon an old, worn Uno deck buried in a forgotten backpack. The find had triggered memories of playing the game with my mom and Fuzz during family camping trips. So, naturally, I'd wanted Maddie to share in that tradition.

For the next year, our Friday nights had revolved around Uno games at the kitchen table. No matter what chaos life threw at us, Friday Uno nights became sacred family time.

For a fleeting second, I wondered what it would be like to give my marriage to Kevin another chance. Would it bring back that warm, homey feeling of Friday Uno nights?

I knew the answer to that question. If nothing else, I'd learned that you can't go back. You can visit places you used to call home, but they're never the same. Whether you like it or not, you've changed, and so have those places.

Maddie won the card game, retaining her status as

reigning Uno champ. Although the night had reached its natural end, it seemed none of us wanted to be the one to break the spell.

"Look, Honey, I regret what happened earlier. I hope it didn't cause any problems between you and Sam," Kevin finally said.

I thought I misheard him. Was Kevin actually apologizing?

"Well, I appreciate the apology, Kevin, but Sam and I are probably over."

"Really? I thought you guys were serious," Maddie said, shooting a disapproving glance at Kevin, who squirmed in his seat.

"Don't worry, it's not because of the argument you had with him," I reassured him. It's something else."

I relayed Annie's news about Big Ted's plan to cancel the festival, then shared that a neighbor saw Tawny leave Sam's house multiple times. Saying it out loud made it feel even more real.

"Do you honestly think Sam and Tawny were involved in something illegal, Mom?" Maddie asked, skeptical.

"Annie reported it to Big Ted, and the police are on it. Regardless, it looks like Sam and Tawny had some kind of romantic thing going on. It lines up. I mean, George suspected Tawny was cheating, and even hired a PI to dig into it."

Maddie shook her head, unconvinced. "Okay, let's assume they were an item. It might have happened before you and Sam even met."

"Maybe," I said. "Either way, he's not who I thought he was."

"I'm sorry, Honey," Kevin said, his tone surprisingly heartfelt. "Maddie told me about Sam, and he sounds like the real deal. I meant what I said about wanting to try again, but mostly, I just want you to be happy."

Kevin's sudden transformation into an emotionally mature human being was freaking me out. Even so, I appreciated the effort and tapped his hand in a clearly platonic gesture of gratitude.

Maddie put her arm around me. "We'll get through this, Mom," she said. "We just have to keep the faith."

I forced a small smile. Keeping the faith was great, but it was going to take a lot more than good intentions and a positive attitude to fix this mess.

## CHAPTER 26

*R*aindrops pattered on the cabin's metal roof as I lay in bed the next morning, promising a soggy Friday. After leaving Maddie and Kevin the night before, I'd returned to my cabin to find a note from Evie stuck to the fridge. "Spending the night at Fuzz's place. See you tomorrow!" There was a smiley face scribbled next to the word "tomorrow."

Evie never used smiley faces, not even in her text messages. She'd gone out of her way to make me feel better about the fact that my boyfriend had potentially shagged our murder victim.

It was time to face reality. Coming home to an empty cabin was my new normal. With Evie and Fuzz's relationship out in the open, she would start spending nights at his cabin, and I'd be eating Lean Cuisines alone in front of the TV.

I didn't blame Evie for wanting to spend more time with Fuzz. Until recently, I thought I'd be spending a lot more time with Sam. Now I was living on my own again, regardless of whether I returned to Rochester at the end of the summer.

There were worse things than living alone. Kevin and I had led separate lives for the last five years of our marriage. Back then, I'd realized I had two options. I could either wallow in self-pity or find something worthwhile to occupy my time.

Birdwatching had been my something worthwhile. With Sam out of the picture, I was looking forward to spending more time rambling around the countryside with a pair of binoculars around my neck. I also had a birding festival to pull off and a lodge to turn around. My plate was plenty full.

To calm my thoughts, I decided to clean the cabin. Evie and I kept our shared spaces tidy, but there was a pile of laundry screaming for my attention in the corner of my bedroom closet. After a quick shower, I loaded my whites into our compact washing machine then moved on to the bedroom and bathroom, giving them both a quick cleaning. By eight-thirty, my whites were in the dryer, my darks were in the washer, and my life was feeling a little more organized.

Next, I brewed a pot of coffee and filled up a super-sized travel mug. I was about to head to the lodge when someone knocked at the door. I assumed Evie had forgotten her keys again, so I opened the door with a smile on my face. My expression did a one-eighty when I realized it was Sam.

"Go home, Sam," I said.

"I just need a minute," he pleaded. "Let me say what I came to say, and if you still want me to go, you'll never see me again."

I wanted to slam the door in his face, but my conscience told me I needed to resolve this. I already had one ex struggling to find closure. I didn't need another one.

"Fine," I said. "You have one minute."

He handed me a manilla folder. "You don't even have to talk," he said. "Just take a look at this."

I skimmed through the papers in the folder. "These look like real estate documents," I said, puzzled.

"They're the purchase offer for 112 Meadow Avenue," he said.

That was the house right next to Sam's place in town. "What does this have to do with us?" I asked.

"Before you and I got involved, I asked Tawny to help me buy that house," he explained. "I heard the owners were thinking about selling, and I wanted to get a jump on things before it hit the market—make it a rental property or something."

Suddenly I realized Sam wasn't wrapped up in anything nefarious. He was just trying to buy the house next door, and Tawny happened to be one of the few real estate agents in town.

"Let me get this straight," I said, my tone lightening. "Your connection with Tawny was totally professional?"

"Totally," Sam insisted. "She stopped by the house a couple of times for signatures—one for the initial offer and one for the counteroffer. But that's all there was to it."

I exhaled. "Why didn't you just tell me this before?"

"Honestly, it never came up," he said. "This is Beechtree—everybody knows everybody, and we all do business with one another. At dinner the other night, I did mention that I've had professional dealings with her."

I mentally rewound through our past dinners, remembering the casual comment Sam had made about Tawny during pizza night at Hop House. The pieces fell into place, Sam was telling the truth.

"Wow, I really messed up," I said, feeling my cheeks heat up. "I jumped to conclusions without even giving you a chance to explain."

He leaned toward me with his big blue eyes. "If it's any

consolation, you don't have to say anything. I wasn't joking when I said I'm serious about us. I wouldn't risk that."

"I should've trusted you more," I said, biting my lip.

"Hey, don't beat yourself up," he said, taking my hand. "I probably would've thought the same thing if the roles were reversed."

I grinned. "The pizza was supposed to be an apology for the whole Kevin fiasco."

Sam's eyes lit up. "I lost my appetite after you left and tossed it, so I guess you still owe me a pizza." Sitting down at the kitchen table, he added, "But for now, catch me up on what I missed."

I filled him in on the whole mess—George, Rupert, and Big Ted's determination to shut down the festival.

"Rupert didn't find any evidence that Tawny was having an affair, but George is pretty sure Tawny was involved in something," I said. "Whatever it was may have led to her death."

As our lips were about to meet in what promised to be the mother of all make-up kisses, we were interrupted by another knock at the door.

The look in Sam's eyes dared me to ignore the knock, but given recent events at the lodge, hiding in my cabin didn't seem like a good idea. When I opened the door, I found Evie, wide-eyed and out of breath, her fist raised and ready to knock again.

"You've gotta come with me right now," she panted.

"What's going on?" I asked, a little alarmed.

Her eyes flicked behind me to Sam, and her brow shot up in surprise. I smirked, a silent promise that we'd talk later.

"You have a visitor. And you're not gonna believe who it is."

# CHAPTER 27

*I* tried to pry the identity of my mystery visitor out of Evie, but she insisted it was a surprise. She didn't look worried, so at least it wasn't another crisis. But it left me baffled. Everyone I knew was either already at the lodge or not interesting enough to justify the suspense.

Sam begged off because he was late for work at the mercantile, but he promised to check in with me later. I gave him a quick peck on the lips and followed Evie over to the lodge. When we walked into the great room, we found an older woman standing by the picture window looking out at the lake. Dressed in tan cargo pants and a striking pink hiking shirt over a baby-blue tee, she was impossible to miss.

"Nora? Is that you? What are you doing here?" I asked, caught off guard.

"I'm here for the birding festival, of course," she said. "It's still happening, right?"

"Absolutely," I answered confidently, knowing Big Ted might pull the plug on the festival any minute. "But I thought you made other plans after our unknown caller threw a wrench in things."

147

"I did," she admitted. "Then I saw all the buzz about the festival online. I've championed women birders for over thirty years, and when I heard you all were shining a spotlight on them, I had to be here."

I told Nora that Evie was the brains behind our publicity. As usual, Evie downplayed her role, but she'd worked tirelessly to spread the word. If the festival was a success, we'd have her to thank for it.

"I just got the ball rolling," Evie blushed. "The other birders spread the word."

Evie and I showed Nora the lodge, then put on our rain gear for a short hike around the grounds. Though the rain had let up, the sky looked ominous.

As we walked, Evie and I shared our vision for Loon Lodge and described how the birding festival was only the beginning. Nora seemed impressed by our ideas and even suggested the lodge could help put Beechtree on the map as a birding hotspot. By the time we reached Warblers' End, Evie and I were floating on air, energized by the possibilities.

Evie pointed to the marsh. "This is Warblers' End," she said proudly. "It might not look like much, but it's one of the best birding spots in the area." She went on to list the various species we'd seen there over the past few months.

"You might have heard there was an incident here earlier this week," I said.

Nora's tone turned serious. "I did hear something about that."

I told her about Tawny, wincing when I mentioned the possibility of foul play. "The police are still investigating, but we're convinced it was an isolated incident." I conveniently left out the part about Betsy's unfortunate encounter.

"It won't affect the festival," Evie quickly added. Then she steered the conversation back to the lodge's picturesque setting and the birds we'd encountered.

Continuing on, I ran through the festival agenda, confirming that Nora was still on to deliver the keynote. It turned out that she had already revamped her talk to include not just Adirondack birds, but also her own journey as a woman in the field of birding. Between making things right with Sam and learning that Nora was still committed to the festival, my day was off to a fantastic start.

Nora flashed a broad grin. "How about I help you get ready for the festival?"

Her offer was incredibly generous, especially for someone as busy as she was. Even so, we had a mountain of tasks ahead of us, so we gratefully welcomed her aboard.

We ended our walk at Fuzz's cabin just as he and Charley ambled out the door. "Well, well, who's this lovely lady?" Fuzz asked, his eyes promising mischief.

Catching Nora's puzzled glance, I mouthed that I would fill her in later.

"You know who I am, you old coot," Evie yelled. "Now, get over here, there's someone we want you to meet."

A fresh burst of rain sent us scuttling for cover under the cabin's porch overhang. "Fuzz Stillman, this is Nora Pruitt, birding aficionado and our festival's keynote speaker," I said.

Nora extended a hand toward Fuzz. "Nice to meet you."

"Welcome to Loon Lodge, Nora. I hear you're quite the bird whisperer!" Fuzz grinned and gave her hand a big shake. "I hope these two warned you about the mosquitoes. They grow as big as hummingbirds around here, and they love a good peck!"

Always the charmer, Charley sidled up to Nora, and she gave him a good scratch behind the ears. He was in doggie heaven.

Fuzz peeked at the sky from beneath the overhang. "Today's a washout, but the forecast for tomorrow sounds promising. Breezy but sunny—perfect for the festival."

I shuddered at the thought of a strong gust sending a vendor's tent soaring across the lawn. I needed to retrieve the tent stakes from Betsy's place as soon as I had a chance.

"Clock's ticking, folks," Evie said, rallying us into action. "Nora and I are headed to the lodge to start setting up displays in the great room."

"Sounds like a plan. Honey and I can grab the folding tables from the storage shed and bring them over to the lodge," Fuzz said. "Come on, Charley."

Charley reluctantly left Nora and followed Fuzz and me to the shed. When Fuzz swung open the shed's rickety door, I caught a glimpse of several folding tables buried beneath a pile of clutter and lawn gadgets.

"All right," Fuzz mumbled, sizing up the jumble of stuff. "Give me a minute or two to dig out these tables."

Perfect. I only needed a few minutes to fetch those tent stakes. "Mind if I dart off for a quick errand? Meet you back here in fifteen?"

"Go for it," Fuzz called over his shoulder as he started untangling hoses and sprinkler attachments.

The path to Betsy's house started just beyond Fuzz's cabin, and I started down it. Charley came along, fishing for more ear rubs. I rubbed his head, told him to stay, and ventured into the woods alone, following the path.

THE PATH to Betsy's house was just a glorified game trail. Brambles and branches stretched across it, and the thick canopy made it seem like nighttime, even on sunny days. On overcast days like today, the mood felt downright gloomy.

Stopping to free a thorn snagged in my shirt, I remembered Betsy was still in the hospital recovering from her attack at Warblers' End. I reached for my phone to call her, then realized I'd left it in the cabin when Evie whisked me away to greet Nora. I should have turned around then and there, but I figured Betsy would understand given the circumstances.

Arriving at her house, I pressed the smart doorbell, half-expecting she would get an alert on her cell phone and give me a chance to explain via the intercom. Nothing. Time for Plan B.

Growing up, I'd spent a decent amount of time at Betsy's house, and I knew her family used to stash a spare key under the birdbath pedestal. I had a hunch that Betsy had kept up the tradition, so I checked beneath the birdbath and bingo, there it was. Grinning, I snatched the key and let myself in through the front door.

Worn floorboards groaned under my weight as I stepped from the small foyer into the living room. Vintage furniture filled the space, and knickknacks cluttered nearly every surface. A musty blend of dust and mothballs filled the air, and the whole scene screamed retro, like time had somehow stopped in the late eighties.

A glance at the bookshelf reinforced my memory of the place. Classics from the likes of Agatha Christie and Arthur Conan Doyle sat front and center—a nod to Betsy's love of a good whodunit. Nestled among them were books on birds and wildlife, reflecting her family's love of nature.

On the middle bookshelf, my eyes landed on a faded photo of our two families standing in front of the fireplace at the lodge. Betsy had just graduated high school, and I must have been seven or eight years old. In the photo, she rocked a tie-dye crop top and a pair of high-waisted blue jeans, the epitome of cool.

I smiled, remembering the day the photo was taken. Back then, I'd looked up to Betsy like an older sister, and I could still picture myself decked out in a homemade tie-dye t-shirt, trying my best to imitate her style.

I moved on to the kitchen and found the bundle of tent stakes on the table, exactly where Betsy had said they were. When I turned to leave, a charming set of porcelain birds on a kitchen shelf caught my attention. As I went in for a closer look, I noticed movement out of the corner of my eye and nearly jumped out of my skin when Mr. Whiskers leapt to the floor from the top of the fridge.

With Betsy stuck in the hospital, the poor cat was probably starving. The empty food dish on the floor beside the fridge all but confirmed my suspicion.

A quick survey of the kitchen didn't turn up any cat food, but knowing Betsy, she'd have something stashed away to tide the little guy over. When I opened the pantry door, I hit the motherlode—a ridiculous stockpile of canned goods. There had to be a tin of tuna in there somewhere.

As my eyes scanned the pantry, I stopped cold. There, tucked in a corner, sat a case of Dancing Daisy sparkling wine.

And one bottle was missing.

# CHAPTER 28

*I* tried to convince myself that stumbling across the same cheap brand of sparkling wine as the empty bottle we found at Warblers' End was a fluke. But what if it wasn't? One way or another, I had to know for sure.

Spotting a can of tuna on the pantry shelf, I dumped its contents into Mr. Whiskers' dish and filled his water bowl, then started searching the house for more evidence.

After striking out in the kitchen, I decided to focus on Betsy's home office. If I didn't find anything there, I'd move on to her bedroom and then circle back to the living room.

Betsy's office was only an office in the technical sense of the word. It was really just a spare bedroom she had outfitted with a reclaimed metal desk and folding chair. An ancient pen holder that belonged in a 1970s workplace sat on the desk, flanked by a vintage snow globe and a plug-in calculator.

The desk's drawers overflowed with personal documents and office supplies. I sifted through the clutter, and in the top drawer, I found a cell phone nestled beneath a mound of old appliance manuals. The battery was dead, but the sparkly pink case identified its owner. The phone matched the description of Tawny's cell phone. Combined with the case of Dancing Daisy I'd found in the pantry, it cemented Betsy's connection to Tawny's murder.

I tucked the cell phone back into the desk and continued digging through the remaining drawers. I didn't see anything else incriminating, but as I was about to move on to Betsy's bedroom, I noticed a cardboard tube leaning against the side of the desk. When I unscrewed the plastic cap and shook the tube, out fell a set of blueprints.

Spreading them across the desk, I discovered they were plans for a condominium development that spanned the entire length of our property, from Warbler's End to Fuzz's cabin. The architectural firm's logo and address were in the lower right corner of the first sheet. The company was based in Schenectady, and even though the firm's name didn't ring a bell, the name on the client line was familiar: Betsy Fitzsimmons.

Betsy wanted to develop Loon Lodge into condos? I still didn't understand how Tawny fit into it, but Betsy obviously had big plans for the lodge.

I heard a noise outside and peered through the office blinds. To my amazement, it was Plummet. He was helping Betsy out of the passenger's seat of a beat-up Toyota Corolla. She wore a hospital gown that revealed a bit too much from behind and had a bandage on her forehead.

The rain had picked up again. Plummet backed his car down the driveway, and I watched Betsy dodge raindrops as she hurried toward the front porch. How long had I been snooping around her house? I had no idea. I stuffed the blueprints back into the tube, then hid in the office closet to figure out my next move.

The front door creaked open and closed, then silence. I assumed Betsy was moving around the living room and kitchen, but I couldn't tell for sure. She was surprisingly quiet for a senior citizen nursing a serious head wound.

An eternity later, the floorboards groaned as Betsy shuffled down the hallway. I held my breath and hoped for the best, only daring to exhale after I heard her trudge past the office to her bedroom at the end of the hall.

I stepped out of the closet and cautiously peered into the hallway. Betsy was singing an off-key version of a tune from "Oklahoma!" in her bedroom. This was my chance. I tiptoed down the hall, my pulse quickening with each step. At the front door, I prayed the hinge wouldn't squeak and slowly pulled it open.

"Find what you were looking for, Honey?"

At that point, I had two choices: I could make a run for it or play it cool. Since I wasn't about to tell Betsy that I knew about Tawny and the condos, I decided to play it cool.

I spun around to see Betsy leveling a shotgun at me. Her hospital gown was soaking wet, and the bandage dangled precariously from her forehead. On any other day, I would have burst out laughing. But there was nothing funny about staring down the barrel of a twelve-gauge.

"The doorbell pinged my cell phone as soon as you stepped on the porch," Betsy explained, "but I was in the middle of getting discharged and missed it. By the time I saw the notification, you'd already let yourself in and made yourself at home. I couldn't have that. So, I called an Uber and had Plummet drive me here straight away."

I wasn't ready to give up on talking my way out of this yet. "Woah, Betsy," I said. "I just came by to grab the tent stakes for the festival, but I got distracted by your collection of mystery novels. Put the gun down and let's talk about this."

Betsy cocked an eyebrow. "You expect me to believe you were hiding out in my office looking for tent stakes?"

That's when I realized that playing it cool was a mistake. I should have made a run for it when I had the chance.

"I know you found a lot more than tent stakes," she continued. "What tipped you off?"

"I really did come here for the tent stakes," I said, my shifting my feet nervously. "But while I was scrounging up some food for Mr. Whiskers, I noticed the case of Dancing Daisy in your pantry with a bottle missing—same as the empty bottle Maddie found the morning we discovered Tawny's body at Warblers' End."

"You wouldn't believe how many times I went back to Warblers' End searching for that missing bottle," Betsy said, almost bragging. "Funny enough, that's what I was doing yesterday when I tripped and smacked my head on a stone. Then I realized I could turn it to my advantage. If I acted like a victim, nobody would ever suspect I might be the culprit. Clever, huh?"

I cursed myself for not questioning Betsy's story. There were no witnesses or evidence to support her version of the attack. Maybe if I'd been more skeptical, I could have avoided this nightmare.

"What happens now?" I asked.

"Simple," Betsy said. She had a smug look on her face. "I was released from the hospital and took an Uber home, but I still felt kind of woozy. While I was getting settled, I heard a noise and grabbed my shotgun to protect myself. I found an intruder in my living room and pulled the trigger. Bang! Oh dear, it turns out it wasn't an intruder at all—it was my good friend, Honey Palmer, picking up some tent stakes. A tragic mistake, but completely understandable given my condition. I babbled nonsense to Plummet the whole ride home just to be safe. When Big Ted asks, Plummet will confirm that I wasn't thinking straight."

I didn't disagree with her about her mental state. "I'm

impressed. Did you put as much thought into Tawny's murder as you have mine?"

"Tawny was a spur-of-the-moment thing," Betsy said. "But let me rewind a bit. For years, I've watched your parents sit idly by as the lodge fell apart."

My blood boiled. "That's not fair. Mom and Fuzz put their heart and soul into the lodge!"

"But it wasn't enough, was it?" Betsy went on to say that her parents had left her a sizable inheritance, and when the lodge inevitably closed due to Fuzz's lousy management, she planned to swoop in and buy it for a song.

She also insisted that the lodge was as much a part of her family's history as it was mine. "I practically grew up at the lodge," she said, her voice a combination of nostalgia and bitterness. "Whenever your family needed something, my family helped, no questions asked. It only seems fair that I get a piece of what's left, doesn't it?"

"How does Tawny enter the picture?" I asked.

Betsy shrugged. "I don't know much about real estate, so I promised Tawny a share of the profits to come on board. I just needed help finding architects and contractors and whatnot, but Tawny took it to the next level. Before I knew it, she'd figured out a way to speed up the process by rezoning the lodge. She'd already started driving out the riffraff and replacing them with the kinds of businesses that appeal to city folk. Apparently, that kind of thing helps drive up the price of real estate. Including condos."

"The two of you were thick as thieves. What changed?"

Betsy's expression darkened. "The dinner. When Tawny started talking about the value of the property and how "if she didn't do it, someone else would," I knew what she was up to. She was going to outbid me and buy the lodge herself, leaving me holding a big bag of nothing. That's when I knew I had to do something."

Betsy confessed she had texted Tawny from a burner phone a few hours after the dinner ended, telling Tawny to meet her at Warblers' End right away. That explained why we found Tawny in her nightgown—she'd dashed out of her cabin to meet Betsy. After the deed, Betsy had snatched Tawny's phone to cover her tracks.

"I bought that case of Dancing Daisy to toast with Tawny once we sealed the deal," Betsy said. "Then I brought a bottle to Warblers' End, thinking it might calm her nerves before . . . well, you know."

"What happened next?" I asked, steadying my voice.

"We tussled, and we even fell into the marsh at one point," Betsy continued, a twisted look of pride glinting in her eyes. "But we clawed our way back onto solid ground, and I held her face underwater until she stopped fighting. If she hadn't been so drunk, I don't think I could've pulled it off. Tawny was pretty strong for a pencil-pusher."

Was she actually gloating about her murder skills? "Wow," I finally muttered. "That's quite the tale."

I could see she was pleased with herself. "I know, right? But sometimes you just have to roll up your sleeves and get the job done," she said.

"I've gotta hand it to you, Betsy. You've thought of everything, haven't you?"

She nodded. "I suppose I have. But let's cut the chitchat. Now, I need you to move a few steps forward. It's not essential, but I think it's better if you go down in the center of the room. Looks more threatening than if you're halfway out the door."

I took a couple of steps toward the middle of the living room, leaving the door open behind me. The breeze felt comforting, calming even. If these were my last moments on earth, at least I'd have the wind at my back.

"It's not personal, Honey," Betsy said, raising the shotgun

to her shoulder. "To be honest, I've enjoyed having you around these past few months. If it makes you feel any better, I think your festival would have been a big hit."

Suddenly, an eighty-pound blur of fur dashed through the door and barreled into Betsy, knocking her to the ground.

Charley lunged at Betsy's calf and bit down hard, eliciting a scream of pain. I took advantage of the confusion and rushed toward her, wrenching the shotgun out of her hands with a quick tug. It was over. But to be safe, I kept the shotgun pointed at her as Charley stood nearby, his teeth bared in a menacing growl.

I didn't have a phone, and leaving Betsy unsupervised wasn't an option. I was formulating a plan that involved a ridiculous amount of duct tape and a kitchen chair when Fuzz appeared in the doorway.

"What did I miss?" he asked, his expression a combination of confusion and curiosity.

I sighed. "The part where Charley saved the day."

Fuzz looked at Charley, who was still standing over Betsy. Then, reaching into his pocket, he pulled out a dog treat and tossed it Charley's way. "Good boy."

# CHAPTER 29

*L*uckily, Fuzz had his cell phone with him and dialed 911. Within minutes, Big Ted and his deputies roared up the driveway, sirens blaring and lights blazing.

I still had the shotgun trained on Betsy when Big Ted strode through the door. Fuzz and Charley stood guard nearby, ready to pounce if Betsy made any sudden moves.

With the entire Beechtree police department on the scene, I handed Big Ted the shotgun and told him that Betsy had admitted to killing Tawny. Betsy, of course, denied it all. She maintained that same smug look on her face and said it was my word against hers.

I was furious. But before I could make my case, I heard a familiar voice behind me.

"Sorry I'm late to the party," Childress said, marching past the deputies into the living room. "I was passing through Beechtree when I heard the call come over the radio." She looked around the room. "What's going on here?"

"Betsy confessed to murdering Tawny," I blurted out. "Now she's denying it all."

Childress whistled through her teeth. "Well, that's an interesting development." The tone of her voice sounded as cool as ever.

"It's also a pretty serious allegation," Big Ted said, fidgeting with his duty belt. "Any evidence to back up your story, Ms. Palmer?"

"I might be able to help you with that," Childress cut in. "We found two sets of fingerprints on the bottle you discovered at Warblers' End. One set belonged to Tawny. The other set didn't match any of the prints in our database, but I doubt Betsy's fingerprints are on file. If her prints do match, then the bottle connects her to both Tawny and the crime scene."

"Trust me, they'll match," I said. "But there's something else you need to see."

I told them about the blueprints for the condos I'd found in Betsy's office. Childress retrieved them and quickly located Betsy's name on the client line. Then, I described Tawny and Betsy's plans for the lodge and Betsy's motive for murdering her business partner. I also pointed out that Tawny's efforts to push out local businesses were at least partially motivated by a desire to enhance Beechtree's appeal and drive up the price of the condos. The blueprints weren't a smoking gun, but they corroborated my story.

Fuzz's face turned red with anger as he stepped toward Betsy. "Let me get this straight," he said. "You and Tawny schemed to drive me out of business so you could demolish the lodge and build condos? Your parents must be spinning in their graves!"

Big Ted positioned himself between Fuzz and Betsy and placed a hand on Fuzz's chest to restrain him. "Take it easy, big fella."

"I can see why Tawny wanted to cut Betsy out of the deal," Childress said. "Tawny had the real estate experience and the connections. I'm guessing she could have easily secured her own financing, so she didn't need Betsy's money."

"I also found a cell phone in Betsy's desk that matches the description of Tawny's phone," I said. "When Betsy realized Tawny intended to sideline her, she used a burner phone to text Tawny and arrange a meeting at Warblers' End. If you charge up Tawny's phone, you'll find that text. And I bet that burner phone is somewhere in this house too."

Childress perked up. "That would be helpful. The cellular company has been giving us the runaround on Tawny's phone records. What happened after Tawny received that text?"

I relayed Betsy's description of her confrontation with Tawny. Big Ted had to restrain Fuzz again when I explained that Betsy's alleged attack never happened.

Big Ted shot Betsy a disgusted look. "What about the map we found in her cabin? And that number, '1.35'? If it's not a time, then what is it?"

Betsy had remained uncharacteristically quiet as the evidence mounted against her. She finally found her voice. "One point three five million dollars," she said. "That was my best offer. Every dollar in my bank account."

I didn't see that one coming. The Fitzsimmons had always lived modestly. They drove an old station wagon that seemed perpetually on the brink of falling apart. Who would have thought they had so much money squirreled away?

"Are you saying the lodge is worth over a million bucks?" Fuzz stammered.

Betsy shrugged, her voice flat. "It's probably worth more, but that's all I had."

With a stern look, Big Ted read Betsy her rights and clamped on the handcuffs. Then he nodded to his deputies, signaling them to take her to the cruiser.

Big Ted puffed out his chest, a satisfied grin spreading

across his face. "We'll charge her with first-degree murder, false reporting, and maybe a few other things." In Big Ted's mind, he'd solved Tawny's murder, and I knew he'd be insufferable for weeks. "Everything good on your end, detective?"

"A crime scene unit and another detective are on their way to search the house for the phone and any other evidence that might turn up," Childress said. She extended a hand toward Big Ted. "Sheriff, working with you is an adventure."

Big Ted shook her hand enthusiastically. Then he turned to me and said, "Honey, you'll need to make a formal statement at some point, but no rush."

I reached out to shake Big Ted's hand, but he ignored it and gave me a hug instead. Caught off guard, I hugged him back. On his way out the door, Big Ted stopped to shake Fuzz's hand too. I thought Fuzz might snub him, but he surprised me by accepting the gesture as a peace offering.

Childress registered surprise at Big Ted's sudden display of kindness, but I could only shrug. Big Ted was full of surprises.

No sooner had he left than Maddie rushed through the door. "Mom, are you okay? What happened?"

Childress and I took turns filling her in, with Fuzz offering occasional commentary. When we were finished, Childress put her hand on my shoulder. "You've had a big day," she said.

"You can say that again," I laughed.

"I still can't believe Betsy killed Tawny," Maddie said. "She always seemed so nice."

Nice seemed like overkill, but I understood what Maddie meant. I was still struggling to wrap my mind around it myself.

Childress changed the topic. "At least we can look

forward to the festival tomorrow. It's a shame Nora won't be there though."

"Actually, Nora's back on as the main speaker," I said. "Turns out it was Betsy who made the mystery call to cancel her, but Nora changed her plans again after seeing all the festival buzz online."

Childress' face beamed. Her excitement about the festival was a welcome ray of sunshine on an otherwise bizarre day.

"Speaking of the festival, it won't happen unless I go back to work," I said.

Outside, the muffled wail of a police siren grew louder. "It sounds like my reinforcements are here," she said. "Time for me to go to work too. But I'll see you at the festival."

Maddie had a few things to wrap up at work but she promised to touch base with me later. Then she hopped into her SUV and backed down the driveway.

Fuzz, Charley, and I started back to the lodge through the path in the woods. The sky was still overcast, but the rain had let up.

Rubbing the back of his neck, Fuzz asked, "With all your sleuthing, did you ever suspect Betsy might be the one who killed Tawny?"

I shook my head. "Not for a second. I thought I knew her pretty well."

"Me neither," Fuzz admitted. "People always find a way to surprise you, I guess."

"So, what brought you and Charley to Betsy's house?" I asked.

"Well, you said you'd be back in fifteen minutes and when you didn't show up, I got worried because you're never late. Charley must've sensed something too, because he came back to fetch me and led me right there."

I smiled, relieved. "I'm glad you decided to check on me."

Fuzz grinned. "Me too, kiddo. Me too."

# CHAPTER 30

*E*vie's voice rang out from the living room, "Rise and shine, lady, it's showtime!"

After spending most of yesterday morning dealing with the Betsy situation, Fuzz and I had hustled back to the lodge and thrown ourselves into festival preparations. With Evie busy checking in guests and Sam working at the mercantile, we'd enlisted Nora, Maddie, and Kevin's help and somehow managed to pull it all together.

After we'd buttoned down the lodge for the night, Evie and I decided to spend a cozy evening together in our cabin. Now that Fuzz and Sam were in the mix, there would be fewer girls' nights, so we planned to enjoy every minute of it. We'd uncorked a bottle of wine, tore into a frozen pizza, and gotten lost in a marathon of "Midsomer Murders" episodes before hitting the hay sometime after midnight.

Now it was festival day and my nerves tingled with excitement. I managed to scarf down a Pop-Tart before Evie and I rushed to the festival grounds to direct vendors to their spots. The sky was a brilliant blue, and the air was crisp and invigorating—a perfect setting for a festival.

To our surprise, we found most of the vendors already busy assembling their booths. Nora had taken the initiative and shown them to their designated spots.

I felt a twinge of guilt for relying so much on Nora's generosity. Featured speakers are supposed to receive the VIP treatment, but there was Nora, hustling non-stop for the past two days. On the other hand, she appeared to be having the time of her life. After helping Wanda set up the concession stand, the two of them started greeting vendors and early arrivals, chatting away like classmates at a high school reunion.

Festivalgoers began trickling in, and I stopped by the registration table to check on supplies. Maddie and Liliana had volunteered to staff the table for the first shift, and they were dressed to impress. Maddie wore a rainbow scarf around her ponytail, and both she and Liliana sported t-shirts bearing the festival's logo.

"So far so good," Maddie said, greeting me with a hug. "I think it's going to be a busy day."

"No doubt about that," Liliana agreed. "Everyone was talking about the festival at the Hop House last night. If even half of the people who said they would be here actually show up, we'll run out of supplies by lunchtime."

Before long, I started to think Maddie and Liliana were right. The grounds teemed with people from all walks of life, eager to support women birders. The guided birding hikes were a huge hit, and the festival buzzed with talk about the birding opportunities at the lodge and other spots around Beechtree.

At one point, I joined a guided hike and listened as Evie and Liliana ran through the laundry list of species we'd spotted on the property. The festivalgoers ate it up, hanging on their every word as the two described the appearance and calls of various species.

Stepping away from the hike to assess the parking situation, I crossed paths with Childress. She'd swapped her official uniform for something more casual: hiking boots, cargo pants, and a rolled-up sleeved button-down shirt.

We chatted briefly, and inevitably, the topic shifted to Betsy. Big Ted was holding her at Beechtree jail, and Childress assured me the evidence was airtight. Betsy would almost certainly spend the rest of her life behind bars.

Watching Childress stride away, a smile crept onto my face. Despite the whirlwind of the past week, it hit me that I'd gained a new friend. I had a feeling our paths would cross again soon—though hopefully not in Childress' professional capacity.

By the time lunch rolled around, the festival hummed with activity. Nora had wrapped up her keynote speech, and I was working the concession stand with Annie and Wanda when Sam sidled up to the counter.

"What's tasty?" His eyes darted over the chalkboard menu hanging behind me.

"Aren't you supposed to be manning the mercantile?" I asked.

He grinned. "Yeah, but it was kind of dead, so I locked the place up and put a sign on the door, telling folks to come to the festival."

I whipped together one of Wanda's Cuban sandwiches for Sam and a portobello sandwich for myself. Then I guided us to an empty picnic table for a quick lunch break.

"This is incredible," he said, looking around. "It's bigger than you expected, right?"

"By a long shot," I said. "Even the overflow parking lot is overflowing."

He flashed a proud grin, putting down his sandwich for a moment. "I've got to hand it to you. I know you had your reservations, but you nailed it. You've really put the lodge back on the map."

I took a slug of iced tea. "Don't get too excited. We still have a long way to go, but I appreciate the vote of confidence."

"Well, no matter what you decide to do next, you've given the lodge a fighting chance," he said.

"About that," I started. "I had a conversation with Kevin yesterday afternoon, and we made a decision."

Sam looked worried. "Please tell me you're not giving him another chance."

I chuckled. "No, I'm not that reckless. I told him to put my Rochester house on the market. Beechtree's my home now."

A grin spread across Sam's face. "I'm not exactly neutral here, but I think you're making the right call."

"I think so too," I agreed.

Seizing the moment, I decided to ask for a favor. "Hey, would you mind working the parking lot this afternoon? We're short-staffed."

Sam said yes right away. What I left out was that Kevin would also be there. It was a bit risky, but working together might provide an opportunity for them to mend fences.

As the sun dipped lower, the crowd began to disperse. Vendors folded their tents and packed their wares. By any measure, the day had been a total success.

I found Evie and Fuzz lounging on the front porch. Sliding onto the swing beside them, I spotted Charley, snoozing soundly in the corner. My four-legged hero had earned a nap.

"Wow, what a day, right?" I said, my eyes meeting Evie's.

Her face lit up in a grin that stretched from ear to ear. "Best birding event ever."

Fuzz gave my hand a gentle pat. "You really pulled it off." His gaze shifted to Evie. "We all did."

The three of us sat there for a while, basking in the satisfaction of a job well done.

"I've been thinking about what's next for the lodge," I said, breaking the silence. "Today was a game-changer for us."

Fuzz looked at Evie, and she gave him a small smile. "We're on the same page," he said. "In fact, we've got a proposal for you."

My pulse raced a little bit. Fuzz didn't make proposals. He was more of a "go with the flow" kind of guy.

"Okay, I'm all ears," I said.

Evie grabbed my hand. "Before we get to that, I want you to know that I'm moving to Beechtree too."

I wasn't surprised. Fuzz and Evie were inseparable these days, and I couldn't imagine her leaving Beechtree any time soon. Still, it was comforting to know that I wouldn't be the only one changing my address. I'd have my best friend close by.

As I moved in for a hug, Evie raised a hand to stop me. "Hold on, there's more. I'm also planning to invest some of the proceeds from the sale of my marketing firm in the lodge."

"What? So, you and Fuzz are partners?"

"Yep," Fuzz said. "And we want you to be part of it too."

I was confused. "I thought I was already part of the lodge. I mean, one of the reasons I'm sticking around Beechtree is to help you get the place back on its feet."

Fuzz waved his hand dismissively. "Yeah, yeah, but I'm talking about making it official and giving you a stake in the lodge. You'll inherit my share when I keel over, and we still have to hash out the legal details. But as of today, it's a three-way partnership between you, me, and Evie."

"You're kidding, right?" I exclaimed. "What do I know about owning a business? I'm just pitching in around here."

"You do a lot more than that," Evie said. "You and Fuzz are the heart and soul of the lodge. It just doesn't work without you."

I was speechless. I'd never thought of myself that way before, but I had to admit that it felt good.

"Thanks, Dad." I squeezed his hand. "I'll try not let you down."

Evie ran to the kitchen and returned with a bottle of champagne. I was relieved to see it was the good stuff and not Dancing Daisy. Fuzz popped the cork, and we toasted our partnership as we talked about our plans for the lodge's future.

Eventually, Evie excused herself to finish cleaning up. I was supposed to meet Sam at his camper, but Fuzz persuaded me to hang out on the porch swing just a little while longer.

He put his arm around my shoulders. "What do you think, kiddo? Quite a day, huh?"

"You know, I think Mom would be really proud of us."

"I think so too, Honeysuckle," Fuzz said. I didn't even bother to correct him for calling me Honeysuckle.

As the last sliver of sun slipped beneath the horizon, we listened to the loons calling to each other in the distance. That was the moment I knew I'd finally found my place in the world.

I was home.

# ABOUT ALL-WOMEN BIRDING CLUBS

Your probably noticed that all-women (or women-only) birding clubs feature prominently in *Death at Warblers' End*.

Women-only birding clubs are a great way for women to connect with other female birders and learn from each other in a supportive environment.

These clubs offer a variety of activities, such as field trips, workshops, and social events. They can be a great way to learn about new birding spots, improve your birding skills, and make new friends.

There are many local women-only birding clubs throughout the United States. You can find a list of local clubs by searching online or contacting your local Audubon chapter.

Here are some of the benefits of joining a women-only birding club:

- **Supportive environment**: Women-only birding clubs can be a great place for women to feel comfortable asking questions and learning from other women.

- **Sense of community**: Birding clubs can provide a sense of community and camaraderie for women who share a common interest.
- **Networking opportunities**: Women-only birding clubs can be a great way to network with other women in the birding community.
- **Educational opportunities**: Many women-only birding clubs offer educational workshops and field trips.
- **Fun**: Birding is a fun and rewarding hobby, and joining a birding club can make it even more enjoyable.

If you are interested in joining a women-only birding club, I encourage you to do some research to find a club that is a good fit for you.

Once you find a club that you are interested in, contact the club organizer to learn more about how to join. It's that easy!

# A NOTE FROM BELL

Thanks so much for joining me on this Loon Lodge adventure.

If you enjoyed this book, I'd love to keep you in the loop about upcoming releases, exclusive content, and more. Just sign up for my newsletter at BellamyBeck.com/subscribe to stay connected.

Don't forget to hop on over to Facebook to join my reader community, where you can share your thoughts and theories on the latest mysteries.

For more behind-the-scenes goodies, visit my website at BellamyBeck.com.

Stay cozy, my friend!

# ABOUT THE AUTHOR

**Bellamy Beck** is a mystery writer in Syracuse, NY. Bell's cozy mysteries feature feisty female sleuths, and combine twisty plots with dashes of humor and romance. Away from the keyboard, Bell enjoys birding, kayaking, and trying to keep up with the antics of an ever-so-charming standard poodle named Charlie.

ISBN: 979-8-9894947-0-5 (Ebook edition)

ISBN: 979-8-9894947-1-2 (Paperback edition)

Made in the USA
Middletown, DE
04 August 2024

58503651R00109